Orientations by W. Somerset Maugham

William Somerset Maugham was born on 25 January 1874 and was to become a playwright and novelist of staggering talent. Losing both his parents at age 10, he was raised by a paternal uncle. Maugham eventually trained and qualified as a doctor. The initial print run of his first novel, Liza of Lambeth, published in 1897, sold out so rapidly that Maugham gave up medicine to write full-time.

His life was certainly full, as the short biography at the end of this book will attest to, but it is also a life full of marvellous works and dedication to his art.

Index Of Contents

THE PUNCTILIOUSNESS OF DON SEBASTIAN

I

Xiormonez is the most inaccessible place in Spain. Only one train arrives there in the course of the day, and that arrives at two o'clock in the morning; only one train leaves it, and that starts an hour before sunrise. No one has ever been able to discover what happens to the railway officials during the intermediate one-and-twenty hours. A German painter I met there, who had come by the only train, and had been endeavouring for a fortnight to get up in time to go away, told me that he had frequently gone to the station in order to clear up the mystery, but had never been able to do so; yet, from his inquiries, he was inclined to suspect, that was as far as he would commit himself, being a cautious man, that they spent the time in eating garlic and smoking execrable cigarettes. The guide-books tell you that Xiormonez possesses the eyebrows of Joseph of Arimathea, a cathedral of the greatest quaintness, and battlements untouched since their erection in the fourteenth century. And they strongly advise you to visit it, but recommend you before doing so to add Keating's insect powder to your other toilet necessaries.

I was travelling to Madrid in an express train which had been rushing along at the pace of sixteen miles an hour, when suddenly it stopped. I leant out of the window, asking where we were.

'Xiormonez!' answered the guard.

'I thought we did not stop at Xiormonez.'

'We do not stop at Xiormonez,' he replied impassively.

'But we are stopping now!'

'That may be; but we are going on again.'

I had already learnt that it was folly to argue with a Spanish guard, and, drawing back my head, I sat down. But, looking at my watch, I saw that it was only ten. I should never again have a chance of inspecting the eyebrows of Joseph of Arimathea unless I chartered a special train, so, seizing the opportunity and my bag, I jumped out.

The only porter told me that everyone in Xiormonez was asleep at that hour, and recommended me to spend the night in the waiting-room, but I bribed him heavily; I offered him two pesetas, which is nearly fifteenpence, and, leaving the train to its own devices, he shouldered my bag and started off.

Along a stony road we walked into the dark night, the wind blowing cold and bitter, and the clouds chasing one another across the sky. In front, I could see nothing but the porter hurrying along, bent down under the weight of my bag, and the wind blew icily. I buttoned up my coat. And then I regretted the warmth of the carriage, the comfort of my corner and my rug; I wished I had peacefully continued my journey to Madrid, I was on the verge of turning back as I heard the whistling of the train. I hesitated, but the porter hurried on, and fearing to lose him in the night, I sprang forwards. Then the puffing of the engine, and on the smoke the bright reflection of the furnace, and the train steamed away; like Abd-er-Rahman, I felt that I had flung my scabbard into the flames.

Still the porter hurried on, bent down under the weight of my bag, and I saw no light in front of me to announce the approach to a town. On each side, bordering the road, were trees, and beyond them darkness. And great black clouds hastened after one another across the heavens. Then, as we walked along, we came to a rough stone cross, and lying on the steps before it was a woman with uplifted hands. And the wind blew bitter and keen, freezing the marrow of one's bones. What prayers had she to offer that she must kneel there alone in the night? We passed another cross standing up with its outstretched arms like a soul in pain. At last a heavier night rose before me, and presently I saw a great stone arch. Passing beneath it, I found myself immediately in the town.

The street was tortuous and narrow, paved with rough cobbles; and it rose steeply, so that the porter bent lower beneath his burden, panting. With the bag on his shoulders he looked like some hunchbacked gnome, a creature of nightmare. On either side rose tall houses, lying crooked and irregular, leaning towards one another at the top, so that one could not see the clouds, and their windows were great, black apertures like giant mouths. There was not a light, not a soul, not a sound, except that of my own feet and the heavy panting of the porter. We wound through the streets, round corners, through low arches, a long way up the steep cobbles, and suddenly down broken steps. They hurt my feet, and I stumbled and almost fell, but the hunchback walked along nimbly, hurrying ever. Then we came into an open space, and the wind caught us again, and blew through our clothes, so that I shrank up, shivering. And never a soul did we see as we walked on; it might have been a city of the dead. Then past a tall church: I saw a carved porch, and from the side grim devils grinning down upon me; the porter dived through an arch, and I groped my way along a narrow passage. At length he stopped, and with a sigh threw down the bag. He beat with his fists against an iron door, making the metal ring. A window above was thrown open, and a voice cried out. The porter answered; there was a clattering down the stairs, an unlocking, and the door was timidly held open, so that I saw a woman, with the light of her candle throwing a strange yellow glare on her face.

And so I arrived at the hotel of Xiormonez.

II

My night was troubled by the ghostly crying of the watchman: 'Protect us, Mary, Queen of Heaven; protect us, Mary!' Every hour it rang out stridently as soon as the heavy bells of the cathedral had ceased their clanging, and I thought of the woman kneeling at the cross, and wondered if her soul had found peace.

In the morning I threw open the windows and the sun came dancing in, flooding the room with gold. In front of me the great wall of the cathedral stood grim and grey, and the gargoyles looked savagely across the square.... The cathedral is admirable; when you enter you find yourself at once in darkness, and the air is heavy with incense; but, as your eyes become accustomed to the gloom, you see the black forms of penitents kneeling by pillars, looking towards an altar, and by the light of the painted windows a reredos, with the gaunt saints of an early painter, and aureoles shining dimly.

But the gem of the Cathedral of Xiormonez is the Chapel of the Duke de Losas, containing, as it does, the alabaster monument of Don Sebastian Emanuel de Mantona, Duque de Losas, and of the very illustrious Señora Doña Sodina de Berruguete, his wife. Like everything else in Spain, the chapel is kept locked up, and the guide-book tells you to apply to the porter at the palace of the present duke. I sent a little boy to fetch that worthy, who presently came back, announcing that the porter and his wife had gone into the country for the day, but that the duke was coming in person.

And immediately I saw walking towards me a little, dark man, wrapped up in a big capa, with the red and blue velvet of the lining flung gaudily over his shoulder. He bowed courteously as he approached, and I perceived that on the crown his hair was somewhat more than thin. I hesitated a little, rather awkwardly, for the guide-book said that the porter exacted a fee of one peseta for opening the chapel, one could scarcely offer sevenpence-halfpenny to a duke. But he quickly put an end to all doubt, for, as he unlocked the door, he turned to me and said,

'The fee is one franc.'

As I gave it him he put it in his pocket and gravely handed me a little printed receipt. Baedeker had obligingly informed me that the Duchy of Losas was shorn of its splendour, but I had not understood that the present representative added to his income by exhibiting the bones of his ancestors at a franc a head....

We entered, and the duke pointed out the groining of the roof and the tracery of the windows.

'This chapel contains some of the finest Gothic in Spain,' he said.

When he considered that I had sufficiently admired the architecture, he turned to the pictures, and, with the fluency of a professional guide, gave me their subjects and the names of the artists.

'Now we come to the tombs of Don Sebastian, the first Duke of Losas, and his spouse, Doña Sodina, not, however, the first duchess.'

The monument stood in the middle of the chapel, covered with a great pall of red velvet, so that no economical tourist should see it through the bars of the gate and thus save his peseta. The duke removed the covering and watched me silently, a slight smile trembling below his little, black moustache.

The duke and his wife, who was not his duchess, lay side by side on a bed of carved alabaster; at the corners were four twisted pillars, covered with little leaves and flowers, and between them bas-reliefs representing Love, and Youth, and Strength, and Pleasure, as if, even in the midst of death, death must be forgotten. Don Sebastian was in full armour. His helmet was admirably carved with a representation of the battle between the Centaurs and the Lapithæ; on the right arm-piece were portrayed the adventures of Venus and Mars, on the left the emotions of Vulcan; but on the breast-plate was an elaborate Crucifixion, with soldiers and women and apostles. The visor was raised, and showed a stern, heavy face, with prominent cheek bones, sensual lips and a massive chin.

'It is very fine,' I remarked, thinking the duke expected some remark.

'People have thought so for three hundred years,' he replied gravely.

He pointed out to me the hands of Don Sebastian.

'The guide-books have said that they are the finest hands in Spain. Tourists especially admire the tendons and veins, which, as you perceive, stand out as in no human hand would be possible. They say it is the summit of art.'

And he took me to the other side of the monument, that I might look at Doña Sodina.

'They say she was the most beautiful woman of her day,' he said, 'but in that case the Castilian lady is the only thing in Spain which has not degenerated.'

She was, indeed, not beautiful: her face was fat and broad, like her husband's; a short, ungraceful nose, and a little, nobbly chin; a thick neck, set dumpily on her marble shoulders. One could not but hope that the artist had done her an injustice.

The Duke of Losas made me observe the dog which was lying at her feet.

'It is a symbol of fidelity,' he said.

'The guide-book told me she was chaste and faithful.'

'If she had been,' he replied, smiling, 'Don Sebastian would perhaps never have become Duque de Losas.'

'Really!'

'It is an old history which I discovered one day among some family papers.'

I pricked up my ears, and discreetly began to question him.

'Are you interested in old manuscripts?' said the duke. 'Come with me and I will show you what I have.'

With a flourish of the hand he waved me out of the chapel, and, having carefully locked the doors, accompanied me to his palace. He took me into a Gothic chamber, furnished with worn French furniture, the walls covered with cheap paper. Offering me a cigarette, he opened a drawer and produced a faded manuscript.

'This is the document in question,' he said. 'Those crooked and fantastic characters are terrible. I often wonder if the writers were able to read them.'

'You are fortunate to be the possessor of such things,' I remarked.

He shrugged his shoulders.

'What good are they? I would sooner have fifty pesetas than this musty parchment.'

An offer! I quickly reckoned it out into English money. He would doubtless have taken less, but I felt a certain delicacy in bargaining with a duke over his family secrets....

'Do you mean it? May I, er -'

He sprang towards me.

'Take it, my dear sir, take it. Shall I give you a receipt?'

And so, for thirty-one shillings and threepence, I obtained the only authentic account of how the frailty of the illustrious Señora Doña Sodina was indirectly the means of raising her husband to the highest dignities in Spain.

III

Don Sebastian and his wife had lived together for fifteen years, with the entirest happiness to themselves and the greatest admiration of their neighbours. People said that such an example of conjugal felicity was not often seen in those degenerate days, for even then they prated of the golden age of their grandfathers, lamenting their own decadence.... As behoved good Castilians, burdened with such a line of noble ancestors, the fortunate couple conducted themselves with all imaginable gravity. No strange eye was permitted to witness a caress between the lord and his lady, or to hear an expression of endearment; but everyone could see the devotion of Don Sebastian, the look of adoration which filled his eyes when he gazed upon his wife. And people said that Doña Sodina was worthy of all his affection. They said that her virtue was only matched by her piety, and her piety was patent to the whole world, for every day she went to the cathedral at Xiormonez and remained long immersed in her devotions. Her charity was exemplary, and no beggar ever applied to her in vain.

But even if Don Sebastian and his wife had not possessed these conjugal virtues, they would have been in Xiormonez persons of note, since not only did they belong to an old and respected family, which was rich as well, but the gentleman's brother was archbishop of the See, who, when he graced the cathedral city with his presence, paid the greatest attention to Don Sebastian and Doña Sodina. Everyone said that the Archbishop Pablo would shortly become a cardinal, for he was a great favourite with the king, and with the latter His Holiness the Pope was then on terms of quite unusual friendship.

And in those days, when the priesthood was more noticeable for its gallantry than for its good works, it was refreshing to find so high-placed a dignitary of the Church a pattern of Christian virtues, who, notwithstanding his gorgeous habit of life, his retinue, his palaces, recalled, by his freedom from at least two of the seven deadly sins, the simplicity of the apostles, which the common people have often supposed the perfect state of the minister of God.

Don Sebastian had been affianced to Doña Sodina when he was a boy of ten, and before she could properly pronounce the viperish sibilants of her native tongue. When the lady attained her sixteenth year, the pair were solemnly espoused, and the young priest Pablo, the bridegroom's brother, assisted at the ceremony. In these days the union would have been instanced as a triumphant example of the success of the mariage de convenance, but at that time such arrangements were so usual that it never occurred to anyone to argue for or against them. Yet it was not customary for a young man of two-and-twenty to fall madly in love with the bride whom he saw for the first time a day or two before his marriage, and it was still less customary for the bride to give back an equal affection. For fifteen years the couple lived in harmony and contentment, with nothing to trouble the even tenor of their lives; and if there was a cloud in their sky, it was that a kindly Providence had vouchsafed no fruit to the union, notwithstanding the prayers and candles which Doña Sodina was known to have offered at the shrine of more than one saint in Spain who had made that kind of miracle particularly his own.

But even felicitous marriages cannot last for ever, since if the love does not die the lovers do. And so it came to pass that Doña Sodina, having eaten excessively of pickled shrimps, which the abbess of a highly respected convent had assured her were of great efficacy in the begetting of children, took a fever of the stomach, as the chronicle inelegantly puts it, and after a week of suffering was called to the other world, from which, as from the pickled shrimps, she had always expected much. There let us hope her virtues have been rewarded, and she rests in peace and happiness.

IV

When Don Sebastian walked from the cathedral to his house after the burial of his wife, no one saw a trace of emotion on his face, and it was with his wonted grave courtesy that he bowed to a friend as he passed him. Sternly and briefly, as usual, he gave orders that no one should disturb him, and went to the room of Doña Sodina; he knelt on the praying-stool which Doña Sodina had daily used for so many years, and he fixed his eyes on the crucifix hanging on the wall above it. The day passed, and the night passed, and Don Sebastian never moved, no thought or emotion entered him; being alive, he was like the dead; he was like the dead that linger on the outer limits of hell, with never a hope for the future, dull with the despair that shall last forever and ever and ever. But when the woman who had nursed him in his childhood lovingly disobeyed his order and entered to give him food, she saw no tear in his eye, no sign of weeping.

'You are right!' he said, painfully rising from his knees. 'Give me to eat.'

Listlessly taking the food, he sank into a chair and looked at the bed on which had lately rested the corpse of Doña Sodina; but a kindly nature relieved his unhappiness, and he fell into a weary sleep.

When he awoke, the night was far advanced; the house, the town were filled with silence; all round him was darkness, and the ivory crucifix shone dimly, dimly. Outside the door a page was sleeping;

he woke him and bade him bring light.... In his sorrow, Don Sebastian began to look at the things his wife had loved; he fingered her rosary, and turned over the pages of the half-dozen pious books which formed her library; he looked at the jewels which he had seen glittering on her bosom; the brocades, the rich silks, the cloths of gold and silver that she had delighted to wear. And at last he came across an old breviary which he thought she had lost, how glad she would have been to find it, she had so often regretted it! The pages were musty with their long concealment, and only faintly could be detected the scent which Doña Sodina used yearly to make and strew about her things. Turning over the pages listlessly, he saw some crabbed writing; he took it to the light, 'To-night, my beloved, I come.' And the handwriting was that of Pablo, Archbishop of Xiormonez. Don Sebastian looked at it long. Why should his brother write such words in the breviary of Doña Sodina? He turned the pages and the handwriting of his wife met his eye and the words were the same, 'To-night, my beloved, I come', as if they were such delight to her that she must write them herself. The breviary dropped from Don Sebastian's hand.

The taper, flickering in the draught, threw glaring lights on Don Sebastian's face, but it showed no change in it. He sat looking at the fallen breviary, and, in his mind, at the love which was dead. At last he passed his hand over his forehead.

'And yet,' he whispered, 'I loved thee well!'

But as the day came he picked up the breviary and locked it in a casket; he knelt again at the praying-stool and, lifting his hands to the crucifix, prayed silently. Then he locked the door of Doña Sodina's room, and it was a year before he entered it again.

That day the Archbishop Pablo came to his brother to offer consolation for his loss, and Don Sebastian at the parting kissed him on either cheek.

V

The people of Xiormonez said that Don Sebastian was heart-broken, for from the date of his wife's interment he was not seen in the streets by day. A few, returning home from some riot, had met him wandering in the dead of the night, but he passed them silently by. But he sent his servants to Toledo and Burgos, to Salamanca, Cordova, even to Paris and Rome; and from all these places they brought him books, and day after day he studied in them, till the common folk asked if he had turned magician.

So passed eleven months, and nearly twelve, till it wanted but five days to the anniversary of the death of Doña Sodina. Then Don Sebastian wrote to his brother the letter which for months he had turned over in his mind,

'Seeing the instability of all human things, and the uncertain length of our exile upon earth, I have considered that it is evil for brothers to remain so separate. Therefore I implore you, who are my only relative in this world, and heir to all my goods and estates, to visit me quickly, for I have a presentiment that death is not far off, and I would see you before we are parted by the immense sea.'

The archbishop was thinking that he must shortly pay a visit to his cathedral city, and, as his brother had desired, came to Xiormonez immediately. On the anniversary of Doña Sodina's interment, Don Sebastian entertained Archbishop Pablo to supper.

'My brother,' said he, to his guest, 'I have lately received from Cordova a wine which I desire you to taste. It is very highly prized in Africa, whence I am told it comes, and it is made with curious art and labour.'

Glass cups were brought, and the wine poured in. The archbishop was a connoisseur, and held it between the light and himself, admiring the sparkling clearness, and then inhaled the odour.

'It is nectar,' he said.

At last he sipped it.

'The flavour is very strange.'

He drank deeply. Don Sebastian looked at him and smiled as his brother put down the empty glass. But when he was himself about to drink, the cup fell between his hands and the steward's, breaking into a hundred fragments, and the wine spilt on the floor.

'Fool!' cried Don Sebastian, and in his anger struck the servant.

But being a man of peace, the archbishop interposed.

'Do not be angry with him; it was an accident. There is more wine in the flagon.'

'No, I will not drink it,' said Don Sebastian, wrathfully. 'I will drink no more to-night.'

The archbishop shrugged his shoulders.

When they were alone, Don Sebastian made a strange request.

'My brother, it is a year to-day that Sodina was buried, and I have not entered her room since then. But now I have a desire to see it. Will you come with me?'

The archbishop consented, and together they crossed the long corridor that led to Doña Sodina's apartment, preceded by a boy with lights.

Don Sebastian unlocked the door, and, taking the taper from the page's hand, entered. The archbishop followed. The air was chill and musty, and even now an odour of recent death seemed to pervade the room.

Don Sebastian went to a casket, and from it took a breviary. He saw his brother start as his eye fell on it. He turned over the leaves till he came to a page on which was the archbishop's handwriting, and handed it to him.

'Oh God!' exclaimed the priest, and looked quickly at the door. Don Sebastian was standing in front of it. He opened his mouth to cry out, but Don Sebastian interrupted him.

'Do not be afraid! I will not touch you.'

For a while they looked at one another silently; one pale, sweating with terror, the other calm and grave as usual. At last Don Sebastian spoke, hoarsely.

'Did she, did she love you?'

'Oh, my brother, forgive her. It was long ago, and she repented bitterly. And I, I!'

'I have forgiven you.'

The words were said so strangely that the archbishop shuddered. What did he mean?

Don Sebastian smiled.

'You have no cause for anxiety. From now it is finished. I will forget.' And, opening the door, he helped his brother across the threshold. The archbishop's hand was clammy as a hand of death.

When Don Sebastian bade his brother good-night, he kissed him on either cheek.

VI

The priest returned to his palace, and when he was in bed his secretary prepared to read to him, as was his wont, but the archbishop sent him away, desiring to be alone. He tried to think; but the wine he had drunk was heavy upon him, and he fell asleep. But presently he awoke, feeling thirsty; he drank some water.... Then he became strangely wide-awake, a feeling of uneasiness came over him as of some threatening presence behind him, and again he felt the thirst. He stretched out his hand for the flagon, but now there was a mist before his eyes and he could not see, his hand trembled so that he spilled the water. And the uneasiness was magnified till it became a terror, and the thirst was horrible. He opened his mouth to call out, but his throat was dry, so that no sound came. He tried to rise from his bed, but his limbs were heavy and he could not move. He breathed quicker and quicker, and his skin was extraordinarily dry. The terror became an agony; it was unbearable. He wanted to bury his face in the pillows to hide it from him; he felt the hair on his head hard and dry, and it stood on end! He called to God for help, but no sound came from his mouth. Then the terror took shape and form, and he knew that behind him was standing Doña Sodina, and she was looking at him with terrible, reproachful eyes. And a second Doña Sodina came and stood at the end of the bed, and another came by her side, and the room was filled with them. And his thirst was horrible; he tried to moisten his mouth with spittle, but the source of it was dry. Cramps seized his limbs, so that he writhed with pain. Presently a red glow fell upon the room and it became hot and hotter, till he gasped for breath; it blinded him, but he could not close his eyes. And he knew it was the glow of hell-fire, for in his ears rang the groans of souls in torment, and among the voices he recognised that of Doña Sodina, and then, then he heard his own voice. And, in the livid heat, he saw himself in his episcopal robes, lying on the ground, chained to Doña Sodina, hand and foot. And he knew that as long as heaven and earth should last, the torment of hell would continue.

When the priests came in to their master in the morning, they found him lying dead, with his eyes wide open, staring with a ghastly brilliancy into the unknown. Then there was weeping and lamentation, and from house to house the people told one another that the archbishop had died in his sleep. The bells were set tolling, and as Don Sebastian, in his solitude, heard them, referring to the chief ingredient of that strange wine from Cordova, he permitted himself the only jest of his life.

'It was Belladonna that sent his body to the worms; and it was Belladonna that sent his soul to hell.'

VII

The chronicle does not state whether the thought of his brother's heritage had ever entered Don Sebastian's head; but the fact remains that he was sole heir, and the archbishop had gathered the loaves and fishes to such purpose during his life that his death made Don Sebastian one of the wealthiest men in Spain. The simplest actions in this world, oh Martin Tupper! have often the most unforeseen results.

Now, Don Sebastian had always been ambitious, and his changed circumstances made him realise more clearly than ever that his merit was worthy of a brilliant arena. The times were propitious, for the old king had just died, and the new one had sent away the army of priests and monks which had turned every day into a Sunday; people said that God Almighty had had His day, and that the heathen deities had come to rule in His stead. From all corners of Spain gallants were coming to enjoy the sunshine, and everyone who could make a compliment or a graceful bow was sure of a welcome.

So Don Sebastian prepared to go to Madrid. But before leaving his native town he thought well to appease a possibly vengeful Providence by erecting in the cathedral a chapel in honour of his patron saint; not that he thought the saints would trouble themselves about the death of his brother, even though the causes of it were not entirely natural, but Don Sebastian remembered that Pablo was an archbishop, and the fact caused him a certain anxiety. He called together architects and sculptors, and ordered them to erect an edifice befitting his dignity; and being a careful man, as all Spaniards are, thought he would serve himself as well as the saint, and bade the sculptors make an image of Doña Sodina and an image of himself, in order that he might use the chapel also as a burial-place.

To pay for this, Don Sebastian left the revenue of several of his brother's farms, and then, with a peaceful conscience, set out for the capital.

At Madrid he laid himself out to gain the favour of his sovereign, and by dint of unceasing flattery soon received much of the king's attention; and presently Philip deigned to ask his advice on petty matters. And since Don Sebastian took care to advise as he saw the king desired, the latter concluded that the courtier was a man of stamina and ability, and began to consult him on matters of state. Don Sebastian opined that the pleasure of the prince must always come before the welfare of the nation, and the king was so impressed with his sagacity that one day he asked his opinion on a question of precedence, to the indignation of the most famous councillors in the land.

But the haughty soul of Don Sebastian chafed because he was only one among many favourites. The court was full of flatterers as assiduous and as obsequious as himself; his proud Castilian blood could brook no companions.... But one day, as he was moodily waiting in the royal antechamber, thinking of these things, it occurred to him that a certain profession had always been in great honour among princes, and he remembered that he had a cousin of eighteen, who was being educated in a convent near Xiormonez. She was beautiful. With buoyant heart he went to his house and told his steward to fetch her from the convent at once. Within a fortnight she was at Madrid.... Mercia was presented to the queen in the presence of Philip, and Don Sebastian noticed that the royal eye lighted up as he gazed on the bashful maiden. Then all the proud Castilian had to do was to shut his eyes and allow the king to make his own opportunities. Within a week Mercia was created maid of honour to the queen, and Don Sebastian was seized with an indisposition which confined him to his room.

The king paid his court royally, which is, boldly; and Doña Mercia had received in the convent too religious an education not to know that it was her duty to grant the king whatever it graciously pleased him to ask....

When Don Sebastian recovered from his illness, he found the world at his feet, for everyone was talking of the king's new mistress, and it was taken as a matter of course that her cousin and guardian should take a prominent part in the affairs of the country. But Don Sebastian was furious! He went to the king and bitterly reproached him for thus dishonouring him.... Philip was a humane and generous-minded man, and understood that with a certain temperament it might be annoying to have one's ward philander with a king, so he did his best to console the courtier. He called him his friend and brother; he told him he would always love him, but Don Sebastian would not be consoled. And nothing would comfort him except to be made High Admiral of the Fleet. Philip was charmed to settle the matter so simply, and as he delighted in generosity when to be generous cost him nothing, he also created Don Sebastian Duke of Losas, and gave him, into the bargain, the hand of the richest heiress in Spain.

And that is the end of the story of the punctiliousness of Don Sebastian. With his second wife he lived many years, beloved of his sovereign, courted by the world, honoured by all, till he was visited by the Destroyer of Delights and the Leveller of the Grandeur of this World....

VIII

Towards evening, the Duke of Losas passed my hotel, and, seeing me at the door, asked if I had read the manuscript.

'I thought it interesting,' I said, a little coldly, for, of course, I knew no Englishman would have acted like Don Sebastian.

He shrugged his shoulders.

'It is not half so interesting as a good dinner.'

At these words I felt bound to offer him such hospitality as the hotel afforded. I found him a very agreeable messmate. He told me the further history of his family, which nearly became extinct at the end of the last century, since the only son of the seventh duke had, unfortunately, not been born of any duchess. But Ferdinand, who was then King of Spain, was unwilling that an ancient family should die out, and was, at the same time, sorely in want of money; so the titles and honours of the house were continued to the son of the seventh duke, and King Ferdinand built himself another palace.

'But now,' said my guest, mournfully shaking his head, 'it is finished. My palace and a few acres of barren rock are all that remain to me of the lands of my ancestors, and I am the last of the line.'

But I bade him not despair. He was a bachelor and a duke, and not yet forty. I advised him to go to the United States before they put a duty on foreign noblemen; this was before the war; and I recommended him to take Maida Vale and Manchester on his way. Personally, I gave him a letter of introduction to an heiress of my acquaintance at Hampstead; for even in these days it is not so bad a thing to be Duchess of Losas, and the present duke has no brother.

A BAD EXAMPLE

I

James Clinton was a clerk in the important firm of Haynes, Bryan & Co., and he held in it an important position. He was the very essence of respectability, and he earned one hundred and fifty-six pounds per annum. James Clinton believed in the Church of England and the Conservative party, in the greatness of Great Britain, in the need of more ships for the navy, and in the superiority of city men to other members of the commonweal.

'It's the man of business that makes the world go round,' he was in the habit of saying. 'D'you think, sir, that fifty thousand country squires could rule Great Britain? No; it's the city man, the man who's 'ad a sound business training, that's made England what it is. And that is why I 'old the Conservative party most capable of governing this mighty empire, because it 'as taken the business man to its 'eart. The strength of the Conservative party lies in its brewers and its city men, its bankers and iron-founders and stockbrokers; and as long as the Liberal party is a nest of Socialists and Trades-Unionists and Anarchists, we city men cannot and will not give it our support.'

Except for the lamentable conclusion of his career, he would undoubtedly have become an Imperialist, and the Union of the Great Anglo-Saxon Races would have found in him the sturdiest of supporters!

Mr Clinton was a little, spindly-shanked man, with weak, myopic eyes, protruding fishlike behind his spectacles. His hair was scant, worn long to conceal the baldness of the crown, and Cæsar was pleased to wear a wreath of laurel for the same purpose.... Mr Clinton wore small side-whiskers, but was otherwise clean-shaven, and the lack of beard betrayed the weakness of his mouth; his teeth were decayed and yellow. He was always dressed in a black tail-coat, shiny at the elbows; and he wore a shabby, narrow black tie, with a false diamond stud in his dickey. His grey trousers were baggy at the knees and frayed at the edges; his boots had a masculine and English breadth of toe. His top hat, of antiquated shape, was kept carefully brushed, but always looked as if it were suffering from a recent shower. When he had deserted the frivolous byways in which bachelordom is wont to disport itself for the sober path of the married man, he had begun to carry to and from the city a small black bag to impress upon the world at large his eminent respectability. Mr Clinton was married to Amy, second daughter of John Rayner, Esquire, of Peckham Rye....

II

Every morning Mr Clinton left his house in Camberwell in time to catch the eight-fifty-five train for the city. He made his way up Ludgate Hill, walking sideways, with a projection of the left part of his body, a habit he had acquired from constantly slipping past and between people who walked less rapidly than himself. Such persons always annoyed him; if they were not in a hurry he was, and they had no right to obstruct the way; and it was improper for a city man to loiter in the morning, the luncheon-hour was the time for loitering, no one was then in haste; but in the morning and at night on the way back to the station, one ought to walk at the same pace as everybody else. If Mr Clinton had been head of a firm, he would never have had in his office a man who sauntered in the morning. If a man wanted to loiter, let him go to the West-end; there he could lounge about all day. But the city was meant for business, and there wasn't time for West-end airs in the city.

Mr Clinton reached his office at a quarter to ten, except when the train, by some mistake, arrived up to time, when he arrived at nine-thirty precisely. On these occasions he would sit in his room with the door open, awaiting the coming of the office-boy, who used to arrive two minutes before Mr Clinton and was naturally much annoyed when the punctuality of the train prepared him a reprimand.

'Is that you, Dick?' called Mr Clinton, when he heard a footstep.

'Yes, sir,' answered the boy, appearing.

Mr Clinton looked up from his nails, which he was paring with a pair of pocket scissors.

'What is the meaning of this? You don't call this 'alf-past nine, do you?'

'Very sorry,' said the boy; 'it wasn't my fault, sir; train was late.'

'It's not the first time I've 'ad to speak to you about this, Dick; you know quite well that the company is always unpunctual; you should come by an earlier train.'

The office-boy looked sulky and did not answer. Mr Clinton proceeded, 'I 'ad to open the office myself. As assistant-manager, you know quite well that it is not my duty to open the office. You receive sixteen shillings a week to be 'ere at 'alf-past nine, and if you don't feel yourself capable of performing the duties for which you was engaged, you should give notice.... Don't let it occur again.'

But usually, on arriving, Mr Clinton took off his tail-coat and put on a jacket, manufactured from the office paper a pair of false cuffs to keep his own clean, and having examined the nibs in both his penholders and sharpened his pencil, set to work. From then till one o'clock he remained at his desk, solemnly poring over figures, casting accounts, comparing balance-sheets, writing letters, occasionally going for some purpose or another into the clerks' office or into the room of one of the partners. At one he went to luncheon, taking with him the portion of his Daily Telegraph which he was in the habit of reading during that meal. He went to an A. B. C. shop and ordered a roll and butter, a cup of chocolate and a scone. He divided his pat of butter into two, one half being for the roll and the other for the scone; he drank one moiety of the cup of chocolate after eating the roll, and the other after eating the scone. Meanwhile he read pages three and four of the Daily Telegraph. At a quarter to two he folded the paper, put down sixpence in payment, and slowly walked back to the office. He returned to his desk and there spent the afternoon solemnly poring over figures, casting accounts, comparing balance-sheets, writing letters, occasionally going for some purpose or another into the clerks' office or into the room of one of the partners. At ten minutes to six he wiped his pens and put them back in the tray, tidied his desk and locked his drawer. He took off his paper cuffs, washed his hands, wiped his face, brushed his hair, arranging the long whisps over the occipital baldness, and combed his whiskers. At six he left the office, caught the six-seventeen train from Ludgate Hill, and thus made his way back to Camberwell and the bosom of his family.

III

On Sunday, Mr Clinton put on Sunday clothes, and heading the little procession formed by Mrs Clinton and the two children, went to church, carrying in his hand a prayer book and a hymn book. After dinner he took a little walk with his wife along the neighbouring roads, avenues and crescents, examining the exterior of the houses, stopping now and then to look at a garden or a well-kept house, or trying to get a peep into some room. Mr and Mrs Clinton criticised as they went along, comparing the window curtains, blaming a door in want of paint, praising a well-whitened doorstep....

The Clintons lived in the fifth house down in the Adonis Road, and the house was distinguishable from its fellows by the yellow curtains with which Mrs Clinton had furnished all the windows. Mrs Clinton was a woman of taste. Before marriage, the happy pair, accompanied by Mrs Clinton's mother, had gone house-hunting, and fixed on the Adonis Road, which was cheap, respectable and near the station. Mrs Clinton would dearly have liked a house on the right-hand side of the road, which had nooks and angles and curiously-shaped windows. But Mr Clinton was firm in his refusal, and his mother-in-law backed him up.

'I dare say they're artistic,' he said, in answer to his wife's argument, 'but a man in my position don't want art, he wants substantiality. If the governor', the governor was the senior partner of the firm, 'if the governor was going to take a 'ouse I'd 'ave nothing to say against it, but in my position art's not necessary.'

'Quite right, James,' said his mother-in-law; 'I 'old with what you say entirely.'

Even in his early youth Mr Clinton had a fine sense of the responsibility of life, and a truly English feeling for the fitness of things.

So the Clintons took one of the twenty-three similar houses on the left-hand side of the street, and there lived in peaceful happiness. But Mr Clinton always pointed the finger of scorn at the houses opposite, and he never rubbed the back of his hands so heartily as when he could point out to his wife that such-and-such a number was having its roof repaired; and when the builder went bankrupt, he cut out the notice in the paper and sent it to his spouse anonymously....

At the beginning of August, Mr Clinton was accustomed, with his wife and family, to desert the sultry populousness of London for the solitude and sea air of Ramsgate. He read the Daily Telegraph by the sad sea waves, and made castles in the sand with his children. Then he changed his pepper-and-salt trousers for white flannel, but nothing on earth would induce him to forsake his top hat. He entirely agreed with the heroes of England's proudest epoch, of course I mean the middle Victorian, that the top hat was the sign-manual, the mark, the distinction of the true Englishman, the completest expression of England's greatness. Mr Clinton despised all foreigners, and although he would never have ventured to think of himself in the same breath with an English lord, he felt himself the superior of any foreign nobleman.

'I dare say they're all right in their way, but with these foreigners you don't feel they're gentlemen. I don't know what it is, but there's something, you understand, don't you? And I do like a man to be a gentleman. I thank God I'm an Englishman!'

IV

Now, it chanced one day that the senior partner of the firm was summoned to serve on a jury at a coroner's inquest, and Mr Clinton, furnished with the excuse that Mr Haynes was out of town, was told to go in his stead. Mr Clinton had never performed that part of a citizen's duties, for on becoming a householder he had hit upon the expedient of being summoned for his rates, so that his name should be struck off the coroner's list; he was very indifferent to the implied dishonour. It was with some curiosity, therefore, that he repaired to the court on the morning of the inquest.

The weather was cold and grey, and a drizzling rain was falling. Mr Clinton did not take a 'bus, since by walking he could put in his pocket the threepence which he meant to charge the firm for his fare. The streets were wet and muddy, and people walked close against the houses to avoid the splash of passing vehicles. Mr Clinton thought of the jocose solicitor who was in the habit of taking an articled clerk with him on muddy days, to walk on the outside of the street and protect his master from the flying mud. The story particularly appealed to Mr Clinton; that solicitor must have been a fine man of business. As he walked leisurely along under his umbrella, Mr Clinton looked without envy upon the city men who drove along in hansoms.

'Some of us,' he said, 'are born great, others achieve greatness. A man like that', he pointed with his mind's finger at a passing alderman, 'a man like that can go about in 'is carriage and nobody can say anything against it. 'E's worked 'imself up from the bottom.'

But when he came down Parliament Street to Westminster Abbey he felt a different atmosphere, and he was roused to Jeremiac indignation at the sight, in a passing cab, of a gilded youth in an opera hat, with his coat buttoned up to hide his dress clothes.

'That's the sort of young feller I can't abide,' said Mr Clinton. 'And if I was a member of Parliament I'd stop it. That's what comes of 'aving too much money and nothing to do. If I was a member of the aristocracy I'd give my sons five years in an accountant's office. There's nothing like a sound business training for making a man.' He paused in the road and waved his disengaged hand. 'Now, what should I be if I 'adn't 'ad a sound business training?'

Mr Clinton arrived at the mortuary, a gay red and white building, which had been newly erected and consecrated by a duke with much festivity and rejoicing. Mr Clinton was sworn with the other jurymen, and with them repaired to see the bodies on which they were to sit. But Mr Clinton was squeamish.

'I don't like corpses,' he said. 'I object to them on principle.'

He was told he must look at them.

'Very well,' said Mr Clinton. 'You can take a 'orse to the well but you can't make 'im drink.' When it came to his turn to look through the pane of glass behind which was the body, he shut his eyes.

'I can't say I'm extra gone on corpses,' he said, as they walked back to the Court. 'The smell of them ain't what you might call eau-de-Cologne.' The other jurymen laughed. Mr Clinton often said witty things like that.

'Well, gentlemen,' said the coroner, rubbing his hands, 'we've only got three cases this morning, so I sha'n't have to keep you long. And they all seem to be quite simple.'

V

The first was an old man of seventy; he had been a respectable, hard-working man till two years before, when a paralytic stroke had rendered one side of him completely powerless. He lost his work. He was alone in the world, his wife was dead, and his only daughter had not been heard of for thirty years, and gradually he had spent his little savings; one by one he sent his belongings to the pawn shop, his pots and pans, his clothes, his arm-chair, finally his bedstead, then he died. The doctor said the man was terribly emaciated, his stomach was shrivelled up for want of food, he could have eaten nothing for two days before death.... The jury did not trouble to leave the box; the foreman merely turned round and whispered to them a minute; they all nodded, and a verdict was returned in accordance with the doctor's evidence!

The next inquiry was upon a child of two. The coroner leant his head wearily on his hand, such cases were so common! The babe's mother came forward to give her evidence, a pale little woman, with thin and hollow cheeks, her eyes red and dim with weeping. She sobbed as she told the coroner that her husband had left her, and she was obliged to support herself and two children. She was out of work, and food had been rather scanty; she had suckled the dead baby as long as she could, but her milk dried up. Two days before, on waking up in the morning, the child she held in her arms was cold and dead. The doctor shrugged his shoulders. Want of food! And the jury returned their verdict, framed in a beautiful and elaborate sentence, in accordance with the evidence.

The last case was a girl of twenty. She had been found in the Thames; a bargee told how he saw a confused black mass floating on the water, and he put a boat-hook in the skirt, tying the body up to the boat while he called the police, he was so used to such things! In the girl's pocket was found a pathetic little letter to the coroner, begging his pardon for the trouble she was causing, saying she had been sent away from her place, and was starving, and had resolved to put an end to her troubles by throwing herself in the river. She was pregnant. The medical man stated that there were signs on the body of very great privation, so the jury returned a verdict that the deceased had committed suicide whilst in a state of temporary insanity!

The coroner stretched his arms and blew his nose, and the jury went their way.

But Mr Clinton stood outside the mortuary door, meditating, and the coroner's officer remarked that it was a wet day.

'Could I 'ave another look at the bodies?' timidly asked the clerk, stirring himself out of his contemplation.

The coroner's officer looked at him with surprise, and laughed.

'Yes, if you like.'

Mr Clinton looked through the glass windows at the bodies, and he carefully examined their faces; he looked at them one after another slowly, and it seemed as if he could not tear himself away. Finally he turned round, his face was very pale, and it had quite a strange expression on it; he felt very sick.

'Thank you!' he said to the coroner's officer, and walked away. But after a few steps he turned back, touching the man on the arm. 'D'you 'ave many cases like that?' he asked.

'Why, you look quite upset,' said the coroner's officer, with amusement. 'I can see you're not used to such things. You'd better go to the pub. opposite and 'ave three 'aporth of brandy.'

'They seemed rather painful cases,' said Mr Clinton, in a low voice.

'Oh, it was a slack day to-day. Nothing like what it is usually this time of year.'

'They all died of starvation, starvation, and nothing else.'

'I suppose they did, more or less,' replied the officer.

'D'you 'ave many cases like that?'

'Starvation cases? Lor' bless you! on a 'eavy day we'll 'ave 'alf a dozen, easy.'

'Oh!' said Mr Clinton.

'Well, I must be getting on with my work,' said the officer, they were standing on the doorstep and he looked at the public-house opposite, but Mr Clinton paid no further attention to him. He began to walk slowly away citywards.

'Well, you are a rummy old file!' said the coroner's officer.

But presently a mist came before Mr Clinton's eyes, everything seemed suddenly extraordinary, he had an intense pain and he felt himself falling. He opened his eyes slowly, and found himself sitting on a doorstep; a policeman was shaking him, asking what his name was. A woman standing by was holding his top hat; he noticed that his trousers were muddy, and mechanically he pulled out his handkerchief and began to wipe them.

He looked vacantly at the policeman asking questions. The woman asked him if he was better. He motioned her to give him his hat; he put it feebly on his head and, staggering to his feet, walked unsteadily away.

The rain drizzled down impassively, and cabs passing swiftly splashed up the yellow mud....

VI

Mr Clinton went back to the office; it was his boast that for ten years he had never missed a day. But he was dazed; he did his work mechanically, and so distracted was he that, on going home in the evening, he forgot to remove his paper cuffs, and his wife remarked upon them while they were supping. Mrs Clinton was a short, stout person, with an appearance of immense determination; her black, shiny hair was parted in the middle, the parting was broad and very white, severely brushed back and gathered into a little knot at the back of the head; her face was red and strongly lined, her eyes spirited, her nose aggressive, her mouth resolute. Everyone has some one procedure which seems most exactly to suit him, a slim youth bathing in a shaded stream, an alderman standing with his back to the fire and his thumbs in the arm-holes of his waistcoat, and Mrs Clinton expressed her complete self, exhibiting every trait and attribute, on Sunday in church, when she sat in the front pew self-reliantly singing the hymns in the wrong key. It was then that she seemed more than ever the personification of a full stop. Her morals were above suspicion, and her religion Low Church.

'They've moved into the second 'ouse down,' she remarked to her husband. 'And Mrs Tilly's taken 'er summer curtains down at last.' Mrs Clinton spent most of her time in watching her neighbours' movements, and she and her husband always discussed at the supper-table the events of the day, but this time he took no notice of her remark. He pushed away his cold meat with an expression of disgust.

'You don't seem up to the mark to-night, Jimmy,' said Mrs Clinton.

'I served on a jury to-day in place of the governor, and it gave me rather a turn.'

'Why, was there anything particular?'

Mr Clinton crumbled up his bread, rolling it about on the table.

'Only some poor things starved to death.'

Mrs Clinton shrugged her shoulders. 'Why couldn't they go to the workhouse, I wonder? I've no patience with people like that.'

Mr Clinton looked at her for a moment, then rose from the table. 'Well, dear, I think I'll get to bed; I daresay I shall be all right in the morning.'

'That's right,' said Mrs Clinton; 'you get to bed and I'll bring you something 'ot. I expect you've got a bit of a chill and a good perspiration'll do you a world of good.'

She mixed bad whisky with harmless water, and stood over her husband while he patiently drank the boiling mixture. Then she piled a couple of extra blankets on him and went down stairs to have her usual nip, 'Scotch and cold,' before going to bed herself.

All night Mr Clinton tossed from side to side; the heat was unbearable, and he threw off the clothes. His restlessness became so great that he got out of bed and walked up and down the room, a pathetically ridiculous object in his flannel nightshirt, from which his thin legs protruded grotesquely. Going back to bed, he fell into an uneasy sleep; but waking or sleeping, he had before his eyes the faces of the three horrible bodies he had seen at the mortuary. He could not blot out the image of the thin, baby face with the pale, open eyes, the white face drawn and thin, hideous in its starved, dead shapelessness. And he saw the drawn, wrinkled face of the old man, with the stubbly beard; looking at it, he felt the long pain of hunger, the agony of the hopeless morrow. But he shuddered with terror at the thought of the drowned girl with the sunken eyes, the horrible discolouration of putrefaction; and Mr Clinton buried his face in his pillow, sobbing, sobbing very silently so as not to wake his wife....

The morning came at last and found him feverish and parched, unable to move. Mrs Clinton sent for the doctor, a slow, cautious Scotchman, in whose wisdom Mrs Clinton implicitly relied, since he always agreed with her own idea of her children's ailments. This prudent gentleman ventured to assert that Mr Clinton had caught cold and had something wrong with his lungs. Then, promising to send medicine and come again next day, went off on his rounds. Mr Clinton grew worse; he became delirious. When his wife, smoothing his pillow, asked him how he felt, he looked at her with glassy eyes.

'Lor' bless you!' he muttered, 'on a 'eavy day we'll 'ave 'alf a dozen, easy.'

'What's this he's talking about?' asked the doctor, next day.

''E was serving on a jury the day before yesterday, and my opinion is that it's got on 'is brain,' answered Mrs Clinton.

'Oh, that's nothing. You needn't worry about that. I daresay it'll turn to clothes or religion before he's done. People talk of funny things when they're in that state. He'll probably think he's got two hundred pairs of trousers or a million pounds a year.'

A couple of days later the doctor came to the final conclusion that it was a case of typhoid, and pronounced Mr Clinton very ill. He was indeed; he lay for days, between life and death, on his back, looking at people with dull, unknowing eyes, clutching feebly at the bed-clothes. And for hours he would mutter strange things to himself so quietly that one could not hear. But at last Dame Nature and the Scotch doctor conquered the microbes, and Mr Clinton became better.

VII

One day Mrs Clinton was talking to a neighbour in the bedroom, the patient was so quiet that they thought him asleep.

'Yes, I've 'ad a time with 'im, I can tell you,' said Mrs Clinton. 'No one knows what I've gone through.'

'Well, I must say,' said the friend, 'you haven't spared yourself; you've nursed him like a professional nurse.'

Mrs Clinton crossed her hands over her stomach and looked at her husband with self-satisfaction. But Mr Clinton was awake, staring in front of him with wide-open, fixed eyes; various thoughts confusedly ran through his head.

'Isn't 'e looking strange?' whispered Mrs Clinton.

The two women kept silence, watching him.

'Amy, are you there?' asked Mr Clinton, suddenly, without turning his eyes.

'Yes, dear. Is there anything you want?'

Mr Clinton did not reply for several minutes; the women waited in silence.

'Bring me a Bible, Amy,' he said at last.

'A Bible, Jimmy?' asked Mrs Clinton, in astonishment.

'Yes, dear!'

She looked anxiously at her friend.

'Oh, I do 'ope the delirium isn't coming on again,' she whispered, and, pretending to smooth his pillow, she passed her hand over his forehead to see if it was hot. 'Are you quite comfortable, dear?' she asked, without further allusion to the Bible.

'Yes, Amy, quite!'

'Don't you think you could go to sleep for a little while?'

'I don't feel sleepy, I want to read; will you bring me the Bible?'

Mrs Clinton looked helplessly at her friend; she feared something was wrong, and she didn't know what to do. But the neighbour, with a significant look, pointed to the Daily Telegraph, which was lying on a chair. Mrs Clinton brightened up and took it to her husband.

'Here's the paper, dear.' Mr Clinton made a slight movement of irritation.

'I don't want it; I want the Bible.' Mrs Clinton looked at her friend more helplessly than ever.

'I've never known 'im ask for such a thing before,' she whispered, 'and 'e's never missed reading the Telegraph a single day since we was married.'

'I don't think you ought to read,' she said aloud to her husband. 'But the doctor'll be here soon, and I'll ask 'im then.'

The doctor stroked his chin thoughtfully. 'I don't think there'd be any harm in letting him have a Bible,' he said, 'but you'd better keep an eye on him.... I suppose there's no insanity in the family?'

'No, doctor, not as far as I know. I've always 'eard that my mother's uncle was very eccentric, but that wouldn't account for this, because we wasn't related before we married.'

Mr Clinton took the Bible, and, turning to the New Testament, began to read. He read chapter after chapter, pausing now and again to meditate, or reading a second time some striking passage, till at last he finished the first gospel. Then he turned to his wife.

'Amy, d'you know, I think I should like to do something for my feller-creatures. I don't think we're meant to live for ourselves alone in this world.'

Mrs Clinton was quite overcome; she turned away to hide the tears which suddenly filled her eyes, but the shock was too much for her, and she had to leave the room so that her husband might not see her emotion; she immediately sent for the doctor.

'Oh, doctor,' she said, her voice broken with sobs, 'I'm afraid, I'm afraid my poor 'usband's going off 'is 'ead.'

And she told him of the incessant reading and the remark Mr Clinton had just made. The doctor looked grave, and began thinking.

'You're quite sure there's no insanity in the family?' he asked again.

'Not to the best of my belief, doctor.'

'And you've noticed nothing strange in him? His mind hasn't been running on money or clothes?'

'No, doctor; I wish it 'ad. I shouldn't 'ave thought anything of that; there's something natural in a man talking about stocks and shares and trousers, but I've never 'eard 'im say anything like this before. He was always a wonderfully steady man.'

VIII

Mr Clinton became daily stronger, and soon he was quite well. He resumed his work at the office, and in every way seemed to have regained his old self. He gave utterance to no more startling theories, and the casual observer might have noticed no difference between him and the model clerk of six months back. But Mrs Clinton had received too great a shock to look upon her husband with casual eyes, and she noticed in his manner an alteration which disquieted her. He was much more silent than before; he would take his supper without speaking a word, without making the slightest sign to show that he had heard some remark of Mrs Clinton's. He did not read the paper in the evening as he had been used to do, but would go upstairs to the top of the house, and stand by an open window looking at the stars. He had an enigmatical way of smiling which Mrs Clinton could not understand. Then he had lost his old punctuality, he would come home at all sorts of hours, and, when his wife questioned him, would merely shrug his shoulders and smile strangely. Once he told her that he had been wandering about looking at men's lives.

Mrs Clinton thought that a very unsatisfactory explanation of his unpunctuality, and after a long consultation with the cautious doctor came to the conclusion that it was her duty to discover what her husband did during the long time that elasped between his leaving the office and returning home.

So one day, at about six, she stationed herself at the door of the big building in which were Mr Clinton's offices, and waited. Presently he appeared in the doorway, and after standing for a minute or two on the threshold, ever with the enigmatical smile hovering on his lips, came down the steps and walked slowly along the crowded street. His wife walked behind him; and he was not difficult to follow, for he had lost his old, quick, business-like step, and sauntered along, looking to the right and to the left, carelessly, as if he had not awaiting him at home his duties as the father of a family.... After a while he turned down a side street, and his wife followed with growing astonishment; she could not imagine where he was going. Just then a little flower-girl passed by and offered him a yellow rose. He stopped and looked at her; Mrs Clinton could see that she was a grimy little girl, with a shock of unkempt brown hair and a very dirty apron; but Mr Clinton put his hand on her head and looked into her eyes; then he gave her a penny, and, stooping down, lightly kissed her hair.

'Bless you, my dear!' he said, and passed on.

'Well, I never!' said Mrs Clinton, quite aghast; and as she walked by the flower girl, snorted at her and looked so savagely that the poor little maiden quite started. Mr Clinton walked very slowly, stopping now and then to look at a couple of women seated on a doorstep, or the children round an ice-cream stall. Mrs Clinton saw him pay a penny and give an ice to a little child who was looking with longing eyes at its more fortunate companions as they licked out the little glass cups. He remained quite a long while watching half a dozen young girls dancing to the music of a barrel organ, and again, to his wife's disgust, Mr Clinton gave money.

'We shall end in the work'ouse if this goes on,' muttered Mrs Clinton, and she pursed up her lips more tightly than ever, thinking of the explanation she meant to have when her mate came home.

At last Mr Clinton came to a narrow slum, down which he turned, and so filthy was it that the lady almost feared to follow. But indignation, curiosity, and a stern sense of duty prevailed. She went along with up-turned nose, making her way carefully between cabbages and other vegetable refuse, sidling up against a house to avoid a dead cat which lay huddled up in the middle of the way, with a great red wound in its head.

Mrs Clinton was disgusted to see her husband enter a public-house.

'Is this where he gets to?' she said to herself, and, looking through the door, saw him talk with two or three rough men who were standing at the bar, drinking 'four 'arf.'

But she waited determinedly. She had made up her mind to see the matter to the end, come what might; she was willing to wait all night.

After a time he came out, and, going through a narrow passage made his way into an alley. Then he went straight up to a big-boned, coarse-featured woman in a white apron, who was standing at an open door, and when he had said a few words to her, the two entered the house and the door was closed behind them.

Mrs Clinton suddenly saw it all.

'I am deceived!' she said tragically, and she crackled with virtuous indignation.

Her first impulse was to knock furiously at the door and force her way in to bear her James away from the clutches of the big-boned siren. But she feared that her rival would meet her with brute force, and the possibility of defeat made her see the unladylikeness of the proceeding. So she turned on her heel, holding up her skirts and her nose against the moral contamination and made her way out of the low place. She walked tempestuously down to Fleet Street, jumped fiercely on a 'bus, frantically caught the train to Camberwell, and, having reached her house in the Adonis Road, flung herself furiously down on a chair and gasped,

'Oh!'

Then she got ready for her husband's return.

'Well?' she said, when he came in; and she looked daggers.... 'Well?'

'I'm afraid I'm later than usual, my dear.' It was, in fact, past nine o'clock.

'Don't talk to me!' she replied, with a vigorous jerk of her head. 'I know what you've been up to.'

'What do you mean, my love?' he gently asked.

She positively snorted with indignation; she had rolled her handkerchief into a ball, and nervously dabbed the palms of her hands with it. 'I followed you this afternoon, and I saw you go into that 'ouse with that low woman. What now? Eh?' She spoke with the greatest possible emphasis.

'Woman!' said Mr Clinton, with a smile, 'What are you to me?'

'Don't call me woman!' said Mrs Clinton, very angrily. 'What am I to you? I'm your wife, and I've got the marriage certificate in my pocket at this moment.' She slapped her pocket loudly. 'I'm your wife, and you ought to be ashamed of yourself.'

'Wife! You are no more to me than any other woman!'

'And you 'ave the audacity to tell me that to my face! Oh, you, you villain! I won't stand it, I tell you; I won't stand it. I know I can't get a divorce, the laws of England are scandalous, but I'll 'ave a judicious separation.... I might have known it, you're all alike, every one of you; that's 'ow you men treat women. You take advantage of their youth and beauty, and then.... Oh, you villain! Here 'ave I worked myself to the bone for you and brought up your children, and I don't know what I 'aven't done, and now you go and take on with some woman, and leave me. Oh!' She burst into tears. Mr Clinton still smiled, and there was a curious look in his eyes.

'Woman! woman!' he said, 'you know not what you say!' He went up to his wife and laid his hand on her shoulder. 'Dry your tears,' he said, 'and I will tell you of these things.'

Mrs Clinton shook herself angrily, keeping her face buried in her pocket handkerchief, but he turned away without paying more attention to her; then, standing in front of the glass, he looked at himself earnestly and began to speak.

'It was during my illness that my eyes were opened. Lying in bed through those long hours I thought of the poor souls whose tale I 'ad 'eard in the coroner's court. And all night I saw their dead faces. I thought of the misery of mankind and of the 'ardness of men's 'earts.... Then a ray of light came to me, and I called for a Bible, and I read, and read; and the light grew into a great glow, and I saw that man was not meant to live for 'imself alone; that there was something else in life, that it was man's duty to 'elp his fellers; and I resolved, when I was well, to do all that in me lay to 'elp the poor and the wretched, and faithfully to carry out those precepts which the Book 'ad taught me.'

'Oh, dear! oh, dear!' sobbed Mrs Clinton, who had looked up and listened with astonishment to her husband's speech. 'Oh, dear! oh, dear! what is he talking about?'

Mr Clinton turned towards her and again put his hand on her shoulder.

'And that is 'ow I spend my time, Amy. I go into the most miserable 'ouses, into the dirtiest 'oles, the foulest alleys, and I seek to make men 'appier. I do what I can to 'elp them in their distress, and to show them that brilliant light which I see so gloriously lighting the way before me. And now good-night!' He stretched out his arm, and for a moment let his hand rest above her head; then, turning on his heel, he left the room.

Next day Mrs Clinton called on the doctor, and told him of her husband's strange behaviour. The doctor slowly and meditatively nodded, then he raised his eyebrows, and with his finger significantly tapped his head....

'Well,' he said, 'I think you'd better wait a while and see how things go on. I'll just write out a prescription, and you can give him the medicine three times a day after meals,' and he ordered the unhappy Mr Clinton another tonic, which, if it had no effect on that gentleman, considerably reassured his wife.

IX

Mr Clinton, in fact, became worse. He came home later and later every night, and his wife was disgusted at the state of uncleanness which his curious wanderings brought about. He refused to take the baths which Mrs Clinton prepared for him. He was more silent than ever, but when he spoke it was in biblical language; and always hovered on his lips the enigmatical smile, and his eyes always had the strange, disconcerting look. Mrs Clinton perseveringly made him take his medicine, but she lost faith in its power when, one night at twelve, Mr Clinton brought home with him a very dirty, ragged man, who looked half-starved and smelt distinctly alcoholic.

'Jim,' she said, on seeing the miserable object slinking in behind her husband, 'Jim, what's that?'

'That, Amy? That is your brother!'

'My brother? What d'you mean?' cried Mrs Clinton, firing up. 'That's no brother of mine. I 'aven't got a brother.'

'It's your brother and my brother. Be good to him.'

'I tell you it isn't my brother,' repeated Mrs Clinton; 'my brother Adolphus died when he was two years old, and that's the only brother I ever 'ad.'

Mr Clinton merely looked at her with his usual gentle expression, and she asked angrily,

'What 'ave you brought 'im 'ere for?'

''E is 'ungry, and I am going to give 'im food; 'e is 'omeless, and I am going to give 'im shelter.'

'Shelter? Where?'

'Here, in my 'ouse, in my bed.'

'In my bed!' screamed Mrs Clinton. 'Not if I know it! 'Ere, you,' she said, addressing the man, and pushing past her husband. 'Out you get! I'm not going to 'ave tramps and loafers in my 'ouse. Get out!' Mrs Clinton was an energetic woman, and a strong one. Catching hold of her husband's stick, and flourishing it, she opened the front door.

'Amy! Amy!' expostulated Mr Clinton.

'Now, then, you be quiet. I've 'ad about enough of you! Get on out, will you?'

The man made a rush for the door, and as he scrambled down the steps she caught him a smart blow on the back, and slammed the door behind him. Then, returning to the sitting-room, she sank panting on a chair. Mr Clinton slowly recovered from his surprise.

'Woman,' he said, this being now his usual mode of address, he spoke solemnly and sadly, 'you 'ave cast out your brother, you 'ave cast out your husband, you 'ave cast out yourself.'

'Don't talk to me!' said Mrs Clinton, very wrathfully. 'It's bed time now; come along upstairs.'

'I will not come to your bed again. You 'ave refused it to one who was better than I; and why should I 'ave it? Go, woman; go and leave me.'

'Now, then, don't come trying your airs on me,' said Mrs Clinton. 'They won't wash. Come up to bed.'

'I tell you I will not,' replied Mr Clinton, decisively. 'Go, woman, and leave me!'

'Well, if I do, I sha'n't leave the light; so there!' she said spitefully, and, taking the lamp, left Mr Clinton in darkness.

Mrs Clinton was not henceforth on the very best of terms with her husband, but he always treated her with his accustomed gentleness, though he insisted on spending his nights on the dining-room sofa.

But perhaps the most objectionable to Mrs Clinton of all her good man's eccentricities, was that he no longer gave her his week's money every Saturday afternoon as he had been accustomed to do; the coldness between them made her unwilling to say anything about it, but the approach of quarter day forced her to pocket her dignity and ask for the money.

'Oh, James!' she no longer called him Jimmy, 'will you give me the money for the rent?'

'Money?' he answered with the usual smile on his lips. 'I 'ave no money.'

'What d'you mean? You've not given me a farthing for ten weeks.'

'I 'ave given it to those who want it more than I.'

'You don't mean to tell me that you've given your salary away?'

'Yes, dear.'

Mrs Clinton groaned.

'Oh, you're dotty!... I can understand giving a threepenny bit, or even sixpence, at the offertory on Sunday at church, and of course one 'as to give Christmas-boxes to the tradesmen; but to give your whole salary away! 'Aven't you got anything left?'

'No!'

'You, you aggravating fool! And I'll be bound you gave it to lazy loafers and tramps and Lord knows what!'

Mr Clinton did not answer; his wife walked rapidly backwards and forwards, wringing her hands.

'Well, look here, James,' she said at last. 'It's no use crying over spilt milk; but from this day you just give me your salary the moment you receive it. D'you hear? I tell you I will not 'ave any more of your nonsense.'

'I shall get no more salaries,' he quietly remarked.

Mrs Clinton looked at him; he was quite calm, and smilingly returned her glance.

'What do you mean by that?' she asked.

'I am no longer at the office.'

'James! You 'aven't been sacked?' she screamed.

'Oh, they said I did not any longer properly attend to my work. They said I was careless, and that I made mistakes; they complained that I was unpunctual, that I went late and came away early; and one day, because I 'adn't been there the day before, they told me to leave. I was watching at the bedside of a man who was dying and 'ad need of me; so 'ow could I go? But I didn't really mind; the office 'indered me in my work.'

'But what are you going to do now?' gasped Mrs Clinton.

'I 'ave my work; that is more important than ten thousand offices.'

'But 'ow are you going to earn your living? What's to become of us?'

'Don't trouble me about those things. Come with me, and work for the poor.'

'James, think of the children!'

'What are your children to me more than any other children?'

'But -'

'Woman, I tell you not to trouble me about these things. 'Ave we not money enough, and to spare?'

He waved his hand, and putting on his top hat, which looked more than ever in need of restoration, went out, leaving his wife in a perfect agony.

There was worse to follow. Coming home a few days later, Mr Clinton told his wife that he wished to speak with her.

'I 'ave been looking into my books,' he said, 'and I find that we have invested in various securities a sum of nearly seven 'undred pounds.'

'Thank 'Eaven for that!' answered his wife. 'It's the only thing that'll save us from starvation now that you moon about all day, instead of working like a decent man.'

'Well, I 'ave been thinking, and I 'ave been reading; and I 'ave found it written. Give all and follow me.'

'Well, there's nothing new in that,' said Mrs Clinton, viciously. 'I've known that text ever since I was a child.'

'And as it were a Spirit 'as come to me and said that I too must give all. In short, I 'ave determined to sell out my stocks and my shares; my breweries are seven points 'igher than when I bought them; I knew it was a good investment. I am going to realise everything; I am going to take the money in my hand, and I am going to give it to the poor.'

Mrs Clinton burst into tears.

'Do not weep,' he said solemnly. 'It is my duty, and it is a pleasant one. Oh, what joy to make a 'undred people 'appy; to relieve a poor man who is starving, to give a breath of country air to little children who are dying for the want of it, to 'elp the poor, to feed the 'ungry, to clothe the naked! Oh, if I only 'ad a million pounds!' He stretched out his arms in a gesture of embrace, and looked towards heaven with an ecstatic smile upon his lips.

It was too serious a matter for Mrs Clinton to waste any words on; she ran upstairs, put on her bonnet, and quickly walked to her friend, the doctor.

He looked graver than ever when she told him.

'Well,' he said, 'I'm afraid it's very serious. I've never heard of anyone doing such a thing before.... Of course I've known of people who have left all their money to charities after their death, when they didn't want it; but it couldn't ever occur to a normal, healthy man to do it in his lifetime.'

'But what shall I do, doctor?' Mrs Clinton was almost in hysterics.

'Well, Mrs Clinton, d'you know the clergyman of the parish?'

'I know Mr Evans, the curate, very well; he's a very nice gentleman.'

'Perhaps you could get him to have a talk with your husband. The fact is, it's a sort of religious mania he's got, and perhaps a clergyman could talk him out of it. Anyhow, it's worth trying.'

Mrs Clinton straightway went to Mr Evans's rooms, explained to him the case, and settled that on the following day he should come and see what he could do with her husband.

X

In expectation of the curate's visit, Mrs Clinton tidied the house and adorned herself. It has been said that she was a woman of taste, and so she was. The mantelpiece and looking glass were artistically draped with green muslin, and this she proceeded to arrange, tying and carefully forming the yellow satin ribbon with which it was relieved. The chairs were covered with cretonne which might have come from the Tottenham Court Road, and these she placed in positions of careless and artistic confusion, smoothing down the antimacassars which were now her pride, as the silk petticoat from which she had manufactured them had been once her glory. For the flower-pots she made fresh coverings of red tissue paper, re-arranged the ornaments gracefully scattered about on little Japanese tables; then, after pausing a moment to admire her work and see that nothing had been left undone, she went upstairs to perform her own toilet.... In less than half an hour she reappeared, holding herself in a dignified posture, with her head slightly turned to one side and her hands meekly folded in front of her, stately and collected as Juno, a goddess in black satin. Her dress was very elegant; it might have typified her own life, for in its original state of virgin whiteness it had been her wedding garment; then it was dyed purple, and might have betokened a sense of change and coming responsibilities; lastly it was black, to signify the burden of a family, and the seriousness of life. No one had realised so intensely as Mrs Clinton the truth of the poet's words. Life is not an empty dream. She took out her handkerchief, redolent with lascivious patchouli, and placed it in her bosom, a spot of whiteness against the black.... She sat herself down to wait.

There was a knock and a ring at the door, timid, as befitted a clergyman; and the servant-girl showed in Mr Evans. He was a thin and short young man, red faced, with a long nose and weak eyes, looking underfed and cold, keeping his shoulders screwed up in a perpetual shiver. He was an earnest, God-fearing man, spending much money in charities, and waging constant war against the encroachments of the Scarlet Woman.

'I think I'll just take my coat off, if you don't mind, Mrs Clinton,' he said, after the usual greetings. He folded it carefully, and hung it over the back of a chair; then, coming forward, he sat down and rubbed the back of his hands.

'I asked my 'usband to stay in because you wanted to see 'im, but he would go out. 'Owever', Mrs Clinton always chose her language on such occasions, ''owever, 'e's promised to return at four, and I will say this for 'im, he never breaks 'is word.'

'Oh, very well!'

'May I 'ave the pleasure of offering you a cup of tea, Mr Evans?'

The curate's face brightened up.

'Oh, thank you so much!' And he rubbed his hands more energetically than ever.

Tea was brought in, and they drank it, talking of parish matters, Mrs Clinton discreetly trying to pump the curate. Was it really true that Mrs Palmer of No. 17 Adonis Road drank so terribly?

At last Mr Clinton came, and his wife glided out of the room, leaving the curate to convert him. There was a little pause while Mr Evans took stock of the clerk.

'Well, Mr Clinton,' he said finally, 'I've come to talk to you about yourself.... Your wife tells me that you have adopted certain curious views on religious matters; and she wishes me to have some conversation with you about them.'

'You are a man of God,' replied Mr Clinton; 'I am at your service.'

Mr Evans, on principle, objected to the use of the Deity's name out of church, thinking it a little blasphemous, but he said nothing.

'Well,' he said, 'of course, religion is a very good thing; in fact, it is the very best thing; but it must not be abused, Mr Clinton,' and he repeated gravely, as if his interlocutor were a naughty schoolboy, 'it mustn't be abused. Now, I want to know exactly what you views are.'

Mr Clinton smiled gently.

'I 'ave no views, sir. The only rule I 'ave for guidance is this, love thy neighbour as thyself.'

'Hum!' murmured the curate; there was really nothing questionable in that, but he was just slightly prejudiced against a man who made such a quotation; it sounded a little priggish.

'But your wife tells me that you've been going about with all sorts of queer people?'

'I found that there was misery and un'appiness among people, and I tried to relieve it.'

'Of course, I strongly approve of district visiting; I do a great deal of it myself; but you've been going about with public-house loafers and bad women.'

'Is it not said: "I am not come to call the righteous, but sinners to repentance"?'

'No doubt,' answered Mr Evans, slightly frowning. 'But obviously one isn't meant to do that to such an extent as to be dismissed from one's place.'

'My wife 'as posted you well up in all my private affairs.'

'Well, I don't think you can have done well to be sent away from your office.'

'Is it not said: "Forsake all and follow me"?'

Decidedly this was bad form, and Mr Evans, pursing up his lips and raising his eyebrows, was silent. 'That's the worst of these half-educated people,' he said to himself; 'they get some idea in their heads which they don't understand, and, of course, they do idiotic things....'

'Well, to pass over all that,' he added out loud, 'apparently you've been spending your money on these people to such an extent that your wife and children are actually inconvenienced by it.'

'I 'ave clothed the naked,' said Mr Clinton, looking into the curate's eyes; 'I 'ave visited the sick; I 'ave given food to 'im that was an 'ungered, and drink to 'im that was athirst.'

'Yes, yes, yes; that's all very well, but you should always remember that charity begins at home.... I shouldn't have anything to say to a rich man's doing these things, but it's positively wicked for you to do them. Don't you understand that? And last of all, your wife tells me that you're realising your property with the idea of giving it away.'

'It's perfectly true,' said Mr Clinton.

Mr Evans's mind was too truly pious for a wicked expletive to cross it; but a bad man expressing the curate's feeling would have said that Mr Clinton was a damned fool.

'Well, don't you see that it's a perfectly ridiculous and unheard-of thing?' he asked emphatically.

'"Sell all that thou 'ast, and distribute unto the poor." It is in the Gospel of St Luke. Do you know it?'

'Of course I know it, but, naturally, these things aren't to be taken quite literally.'

'It is clearly written. What makes you say it is not to be taken literally?'

Mr Evans shrugged his shoulders impatiently.

'Why, don't you see it would be impossible? The world couldn't go on. How do you expect your children to live if you give this money away?'

'"Look at the lilies of the field. They toil not, neither do they spin; yet Solomon in all his glory was not arrayed as one of these."'....

'Oh, my dear sir, you make me lose my patience. You're full of the hell-fire platitudes of a park spouter, and you think it's religion.... I tell you all these things are allegorical. Don't you understand that? You mustn't carry them out to the letter. They are not meant to be taken in that way.'

Mr Clinton smiled a little pitifully at the curate.

'And think of yourself, one must think of oneself. "God helps those who help themselves." How are you going to exist when this little money of yours is gone? You'll simply have to go to the workhouse.... It's absurd, I tell you.'

Mr Clinton took no further notice of the curate, but he broke into a loud chant,

'"Lay not up for yourselves treasures upon the earth, where moth and rust doth corrupt, and where thieves break through and steal. But lay up for yourselves treasures in heaven, where neither moth nor rust doth corrupt, and where thieves do not break through nor steal."' Then, turning on the unhappy curate, he stretched out his arm and pointed his finger at him. 'Last Sunday,' he said, 'I 'eard you read those very words from the chancel steps. Go! go! I tell you, go! You are a bad man, a wolf in sheep's clothing, go!' Mr Clinton walked up to him threateningly, and the curate, with a gasp of astonishment and indignation, fled from the room.

He met Mrs Clinton outside.

'I can't do anything with him at all,' he said angrily. 'I've never heard such things in my life. He's either mad or he's got into the hands of the Dissenters. That's the only explanation I can offer.'

Then, to quiet his feelings, he called on a wealthy female parishioner, with whom he was a great favourite, because she thought him 'such a really pious man,' and it was not till he had drunk two cups of tea that he recovered his equilibrium.

XI

Mrs Clinton was at her wit's end. Her husband had sold out his shares, and the money was lying at the bank ready to be put to its destined use. Visions of debt and bankruptcy presented themselves to her. She saw her black satin dress in the ruthless clutches of a pawnbroker, the house and furniture sold over her head, the children down at heel, and herself driven to work for her living, needlework, nursing, charing, what might not things come to? However, she went to the doctor and told him of the failure of their scheme.

'I've come to the end of my tether, Mrs Clinton; I really don't know what to do. The only thing I can suggest is that a mental specialist should examine into the state of his mind. I really think he's wrong in his head, and, you know, it may be necessary for your welfare and his own that he be kept under restriction.'

'Well, doctor,' answered Mrs Clinton, putting her handkerchief up to her eyes and beginning to cry, 'well, doctor, of course I shouldn't like him to be shut up, it seems a terrible thing, and I shall never 'ave a moment's peace all the rest of my life; but if he must be shut up, for Heaven's sake let it be done at once, before the money's gone.' And here she began to sob very violently.

The doctor said he would immediately write to the specialist, so that they might hold a consultation on Mr Clinton the very next day.

So, the following morning, Mrs Clinton again put on her black satin dress, and, further, sent to her grocer's for a bottle of sherry, her inner consciousness giving her to understand that specialists expected something of the kind....

The specialist came. He was a tall, untidily-dressed man, with his hair wild and straggling, as if he had just got out of bed. He was very clever, and very impatient of stupid people, and he seldom met anyone whom he did not think in one way or another intensely stupid.

Mr Clinton, as before, had gone out, but Mrs Clinton did her best to entertain the two doctors. The specialist, who talked most incessantly himself, was extremely impatient of other people's conversation.

'Why on earth don't people see that they're much more interesting when they hold their tongues than when they speak?' he was in the habit of saying, and immediately would pour out a deluge of words, emphasising and explaining the point, giving instances of its truth....

'You must see a lot of strange things, doctor,' said Mrs Clinton, amiably.

'Yes,' answered the specialist.

'I think it must be very interesting to be a doctor,' said Mrs Clinton.

'Yes, yes.'

'You must see a lot of strange things.'

'Yes, yes,' repeated the doctor, and as Mrs Clinton went on complacently, he frowned and drummed his fingers on the table and looked to the right and left. 'When is the man coming in?' he asked impatiently.

And at last he could not contain himself.

'If you don't mind, Mrs Clinton, I should like to talk to your doctor alone about the case. You can wait in the next room.'

'I'm sure I don't wish to intrude,' said Mrs Clinton, bridling up, and she rose in a dignified manner from her chair. She thought his manners were distinctly queer. 'But, of course,' she said to a friend afterwards, 'he's a genius, there's no mistaking it, and people like that are always very eccentric.'

'What an insufferable woman!' he began, when the lady had retired, talking very rapidly, only stopping to take an occasional breath. 'I thought she was going on all night. She's enough to drive the man mad. One couldn't get a word in edgeways. Why on earth doesn't this man come? Just like these people, they don't think that my time's valuable. I expect she drinks. Shocking, you know, these women, how they drink!' And still talking, he looked at his watch for the eighth time in ten minutes.

'Well, my man,' he said, as Mr Clinton at last came in, 'what are you complaining of?... One moment,' he added, as Mr Clinton was about to reply. He opened his notebook and took out a stylographic pen. 'Now, I'm ready for you. What are you complaining of?'

'I'm complaining that the world is out of joint,' answered Mr Clinton, with a smile.

The specialist raised his eyebrows and significantly looked at the family doctor.

'It's astonishing how much you can get by a well-directed question,' he said to him, taking no notice of Mr Clinton. 'Some people go floundering about for hours, but, you see, by one question I get on the track.' Turning to the patient again, he said, 'Ah! and do you see things?'

'Certainly; I see you.'

'I don't mean that,' impatiently said the specialist. 'Distinctly stupid, you know,' he added to his colleague. 'I mean, do you see things that other people don't see?'

'Alas! yes; I see Folly stalking abroad on a 'obby 'orse.'

'Do you really? Anything else?' said the doctor, making a note of the fact.

'I see Wickedness and Vice beating the land with their wings.'

'Sees things beating with their wings,' wrote down the doctor.

'I see misery and un'appiness everywhere.'

'Indeed!' said the doctor. 'Has delusions. Do you think your wife puts things in your tea?'

'Yes.'

'Ah!' joyfully uttered the doctor, 'that's what I wanted to get at, thinks people are trying to poison him. What is it they put in, my man?'

'Milk and sugar,' answered Mr Clinton.

'Very dull mentally,' said the specialist, in an undertone, to his colleague. 'Well, I don't think we need go into any more details. There's no doubt about it, you know. That curious look in his eyes, and the smile, the smile's quite typical. It all clearly points to insanity. And then that absurd idea of giving his money to the poor! I've heard of people taking money away from the poor, there's nothing mad in that; but the other, why, it's a proof of insanity itself. And then your account of his movements! His giving ice-creams to children. Most pernicious things, those ice-creams! The Government ought to put a stop to them. Extraordinary idea to think of reforming the world with ice-cream! Post-enteric insanity, you know. Mad as a hatter! Well, well, I must be off.' Still talking, he put on his hat and talked all the way downstairs, and finally talked himself out of the house.

The family doctor remained behind to see Mrs Clinton.

'Yes, it's just as I said,' he told her. 'He's not responsible for his actions. I think he's been insane ever since his illness. When you think of his behaviour since then, his going among those common people and trying to reform them, and his ideas about feeding the hungry and clothing the naked, and finally wanting to give his money to the poor, it all points to a completely deranged mind.'

Mrs Clinton heaved a deep sigh. 'And what do you think 'ad better be done now?' she asked.

'Well, I'm very sorry, Mrs Clinton; of course it's a great blow to you; but really I think arrangements had better be made for him to be put under restraint.'

Mrs Clinton began to cry, and the doctor looked at her compassionately.

'Ah, well,' she said at last, 'if it must be done, I suppose it 'ad better be done at once; and I shall be able to save the money after all.' At the thought of this she dried her tears.

The moral is plain.

DE AMICITIA

I

They were walking home from the theatre.

'Well, Mr White,' said Valentia, 'I think it was just fine.'

'It was magnificent!' replied Mr White.

And they were separated for a moment by the crowd, streaming up from the Français towards the Opera and the Boulevards.

'I think, if you don't mind,' she said, 'I'll take your arm, so that we shouldn't get lost.'

He gave her his arm, and they walked through the Louvre and over the river on their way to the Latin Quarter.

Valentia was an art student and Ferdinand White was a poet. Ferdinand considered Valentia the only woman who had ever been able to paint, and Valentia told Ferdinand that he was the only man she had met who knew anything about Art without being himself an artist. On her arrival in Paris, a year before, she had immediately inscribed herself, at the offices of the New York Herald, Valentia Stewart, Cincinnati, Ohio, U.S.A. She settled down in a respectable pension, and within a week was painting vigorously. Ferdinand White arrived from Oxford at about the same time, hired a dirty room in a shabby hotel, ate his meals at cheap restaurants in the Boulevard St Michel, read Stephen Mallarmé, and flattered himself that he was leading 'la vie de Bohême.'

After two months, the Fates brought the pair together, and Ferdinand began to take his meals at Valentia's pension. They went to the museums together; and in the Sculpture Gallery at the Louvre, Ferdinand would discourse on ancient Greece in general and on Plato in particular, while among the pictures Valentia would lecture on tones and values and chiaroscuro. Ferdinand renounced Ruskin and all his works; Valentia read the Symposium. Frequently in the evening they went to the theatre; sometimes to the Français, but more often to the Odéon; and after the performance they would discuss the play, its art, its technique, above all, its ethics. Ferdinand explained the piece he had in contemplation, and Valentia talked of the picture she meant to paint for next year's Salon; and the lady told her friends that her companion was the cleverest man she had met in her life, while he told his that she was the only really sympathetic and intelligent girl he had ever known. Thus were united in bonds of amity, Great Britain on the one side and the United States of America and Ireland on the other.

But when Ferdinand spoke of Valentia to the few Frenchmen he knew, they asked him,

'But this Miss Stewart, is she pretty?'

'Certainly, in her American way; a long face, with the hair parted in the middle and hanging over the nape of the neck. Her mouth is quite classic.'

'And have you never kissed the classic mouth?'

'I? Never!'

'Has she a good figure?'

'Admirable!'

'And yet, Oh, you English!' And they smiled and shrugged their shoulders as they said, 'How English!'

'But, my good fellow,' cried Ferdinand, in execrable French, 'you don't understand. We are friends, the best of friends.'

They shrugged their shoulders more despairingly than ever.

II

They stood on the bridge and looked at the water and the dark masses of the houses on the Latin side, with the twin towers of Notre Dame rising dimly behind them. Ferdinand thought of the Thames at night, with the barges gliding slowly down, and the twinkling of the lights along the Embankment.

'It must be a little like that in Holland,' she said, 'but without the lights and with greater stillness.'

'When do you start?'

She had been making preparations for spending the summer in a little village near Amsterdam, to paint.

'I can't go now,' cried Valentia. 'Corrie Sayles is going home, and there's no one else I can go with. And I can't go alone. Where are you going?'

'I? I have no plans.... I never make plans.'

They paused, looking at the reflections in the water. Then she said,

'I don't see why you shouldn't come to Holland with me!'

He did not know what to think; he knew she had been reading the Symposium.

'After all,' she said, 'there's no reason why one shouldn't go away with a man as well as with a woman.'

His French friends would have suggested that there were many reasons why one should go away with a woman rather than a man; but, like his companion, Ferdinand looked at it in the light of pure friendship.

'When one comes to think of it, I really don't see why we shouldn't. And the mere fact of staying at the same hotel can make no difference to either of us. We shall both have our work, you your painting, and I my play.'

As they considered it, the idea was distinctly pleasing; they wondered that it had not occurred to them before. Sauntering homewards, they discussed the details, and in half an hour had decided on the plan of their journey, the date and the train.

Next day Valentia went to say good-bye to the old French painter whom all the American girls called Popper. She found him in a capacious dressing-gown, smoking cigarettes.

'Well, my dear,' he said, 'what news?'

'I'm going to Holland to paint windmills.'

'A very laudable ambition. With your mother?'

'My good Popper, my mother's in Cincinnati. I'm going with Mr White.'

'With Mr White?' He raised his eyebrows. 'You are very frank about it.'

'Why, what do you mean?'

He put on his glasses and looked at her carefully.

'Does it not seem to you a rather, curious thing for a young girl of your age to go away with a young man of the age of Mr Ferdinand White?'

'Good gracious me! One would think I was doing something that had never been done before!'

'Oh, many a young man has gone travelling with a young woman, but they generally start by a night train, and arrive at the station in different cabs.'

'But surely, Popper, you don't mean to insinuate, Mr White and I are going to Holland as friends.'

'Friends!'

He looked at her more curiously than ever.

'One can have a man friend as well as a girl friend,' she continued. 'And I don't see why he shouldn't be just as good a friend.'

'The danger is that he become too good.'

'You misunderstand me entirely, Popper; we are friends, and nothing but friends.'

'You are entirely off your head, my child.'

'Ah! you're a Frenchman, you can't understand these things. We are different.'

'I imagine that you are human beings, even though England and America respectively had the intense good fortune of seeing your birth.'

'We're human beings, and more than that, we're nineteenth century human beings. Love is not everything. It is a part of one, perhaps the lower part, an accessory to man's life, needful for the continuation of the species.'

'You use such difficult words, my dear.'

'There is something higher and nobler and purer than love, there is friendship. Ferdinand White is my friend. I have the amplest confidence in him. I am certain that no unclean thought has ever entered his head.'

She spoke quite heatedly, and as she flushed up, the old painter thought her astonishingly handsome. Then she added as an afterthought,

'We despise passion. Passion is ugly; it is grotesque.'

The painter stroked his imperial and faintly smiled.

'My child, you must permit me to tell you that you are foolish. Passion is the most lovely thing in the world; without it we should not paint beautiful pictures. It is passion that makes a woman of a society lady; it is passion that makes a man even of an art critic.'

'We do not want it,' she said. 'We worship Venus Urania. We are all spirit and soul.'

'You have been reading Plato; soon you will read Zola.'

He smiled again, and lit another cigarette.

'Do you disapprove of my going?' she asked after a little silence.

He paused and looked at her. Then he shrugged his shoulders.

'On the contrary, I approve. It is foolish, but that is no reason why you should not do it. After all, folly is the great attribute of man. No judge is as grave as an owl; no soldier fighting for his country flies as rapidly as the hare. You may be strong, but you are not so strong as a horse; you may be gluttonous, but you cannot eat like a boa-constrictor. But there is no beast that can be as foolish as man. And since one should always do what one can do best, be foolish. Strive for folly above all things. Let the height of your ambition be the pointed cap with the golden bells. So, bon voyage! I will come and see you off to-morrow.'

The painter arrived at the station with a box of sweets, which he handed to Valentia with a smile. He shook Ferdinand's hand warmly and muttered under his breath,

'Silly fool! he's thinking of friendship, too!'

Then, as the train steamed out, he waved his hand and cried,

'Be foolish! Be foolish!'

He walked slowly out of the station, and sat down at a café. He lit a cigarette, and, sipping his absinthe, said,

'Imbeciles!'

III

They arrived at Amsterdam in the evening, and, after dinner, gathered together their belongings and crossed the Ij as the moon shone over the waters; then they got into the little steam tram and started for Monnickendam. They stood side by side on the platform of the carriage and watched the broad meadows bathed in moonlight, the formless shapes of the cattle lying on the grass, and the black outlines of the mills; they passed by a long, sleeping canal, and they stopped at little, silent villages. At last they entered the dead town, and the tram put them down at the hotel door.

Next morning, when she was half dressed, Valentia threw open the window of her room, and looked out into the garden. Ferdinand was walking about, dressed as befitted the place and season, in flannels, with a huge white hat on his head. She could not help thinking him very handsome, and she took off the blue skirt she had intended to work in, and put on a dress of muslin all bespattered with coloured flowers, and she took in her hand a flat straw hat with red ribbons.

'You look like a Dresden shepherdess,' he said, as they met.

They had breakfast in the garden beneath the trees; and as she poured out his tea, she laughed, and with the American accent which he was beginning to think made English so harmonious, said,

'I reckon this about takes the shine out of Paris.'

They had agreed to start work at once, losing no time, for they wanted to have a lot to show on their return to France, that their scheme might justify itself. Ferdinand wished to accompany Valentia on her search for the picturesque, but she would not let him; so, after breakfast, he sat himself down in the summer-house, and spread out all round him his nice white paper, lit his pipe, cut his quills, and proceeded to the evolution of a masterpiece. Valentia tied the red strings of her sun-bonnet under her chin, selected a sketchbook, and sallied forth.

At luncheon they met, and Valentia told of a little bit of canal, with an old windmill on one side of it, which she had decided to paint, while Ferdinand announced that he had settled on the names of his dramatis personæ. In the afternoon they returned to their work, and at night, tired with the previous day's travelling, went to bed soon after dinner.

So passed the second day; and the third day, and the fourth; till the end of the week came, and they had worked diligently. They were both of them rather surprised at the ease with which they became accustomed to their life.

'How absurd all this fuss is,' said Valentia, 'that people make about the differences of the sexes! I am sure it is only habit.'

'We have ourselves to prove that there is nothing in it,' he replied. 'You know, it is an interesting experiment that we are making.'

She had not looked at it in that light before.

'Perhaps it is. We may be the fore-runners of a new era.'

'The Edisons of a new communion!'

'I shall write and tell Monsieur Rollo all about it.'

In the course of the letter, she said,

'Sex is a morbid instinct. Out here, in the calmness of the canal and the broad meadows, it never enters one's head. I do not think of Ferdinand as a man'

She looked up at him as she wrote the words. He was reading a book and she saw him in profile, with the head bent down. Through the leaves the sun lit up his face with a soft light that was almost green, and it occurred to her that it would be interesting to paint him.

'I do not think of Ferdinand as a man; to me he is a companion. He has a wider experience than a woman, and he talks of different things. Otherwise I see no difference. On his part, the idea of my sex never occurs to him, and far from being annoyed as an ordinary woman might be, I am proud of it. It shows me that, when I chose a companion, I chose well. To him I am not a woman; I am a man.'

And she finished with a repetition of Ferdinand's remark,

'We are the Edisons of a new communion!'

When Valentia began to paint her companion's portrait, they were naturally much more together. And they never grew tired of sitting in the pleasant garden under the trees, while she worked at her canvas and green shadows fell on the profile of Ferdinand White. They talked of many things. After a while they became less reserved about their private concerns. Valentia told Ferdinand about her home in Ohio, and about her people; and Ferdinand spoke of the country parsonage in which he had spent his childhood, and the public school, and lastly of Oxford and the strange, happy days when he had learnt to read Plato and Walter Pater....

At last Valentia threw aside her brushes and leant back with a sigh.

'It is finished!'

Ferdinand rose and stretched himself, and went to look at his portrait. He stood before it for a while, and then he placed his hand on Valentia's shoulder.

'You are a genius, Miss Stewart.'

She looked up at him.

'Ah, Mr White, I was inspired by you. It is more your work than mine.'

IV

In the evening they went out for a stroll. They wandered through the silent street; in the darkness they lost the quaintness of the red brick houses, contrasting with the bright yellow of the paving, but it was even quieter than by day. The street was very broad, and it wound about from east to west and from west to east, and at last it took them to the tiny harbour. Two fishing smacks were basking on the water, moored to the side, and the Zuyder Zee was covered with the innumerable reflections of the stars. On one of the boats a man was sitting at the prow, fishing, and now and then, through the darkness, one saw the red glow of his pipe; by his side, huddled up on a sail, lay a sleeping boy. The other boat seemed deserted. Ferdinand and Valentia stood for a long time watching the fisher, and he was so still that they wondered whether he too were sleeping. They looked across the sea, and in the distance saw the dim lights of Marken, the island of fishers. They wandered on again through the street, and now the lights in the windows were extinguished one by one, and sleep came over the town; and the quietness was even greater than before. They walked on, and their footsteps made no sound. They felt themselves alone in the dead city, and they did not speak.

At length they came to a canal gliding towards the sea; they followed it inland, and here the darkness was equal to the silence. Great trees that had been planted when William of Orange was king in England threw their shade over the water, shutting out the stars. They wandered along on the soft earth, they could not hear themselves walk, and they did not speak.

They came to a bridge over the canal and stood on it, looking at the water and the trees above them, and the water and the trees below them, and they did not speak.

Then out of the darkness came another darkness, and gradually loomed forth the heaviness of a barge. Noiselessly it glided down the stream, very slowly; at the end of it a boy stood at the tiller, steering; and it passed beneath them and beyond, till it lost itself in the night, and again they were alone.

They stood side by side, leaning against the parapet, looking down at the water.... And from the water rose up Love, and Love fluttered down from the trees, and Love was borne along upon the night air. Ferdinand did not know what was happening to him; he felt Valentia by his side, and he drew closer to her, till her dress touched his legs and the silk of her sleeve rubbed against his arm. It was so dark that he could not see her face; he wondered of what she was thinking. She made a little movement and to him came a faint wave of the scent she wore. Presently two forms passed by on the bank and they saw a lover with his arm round a girl's waist, and then they too were hidden in the darkness. Ferdinand trembled as he spoke.

'Only Love is waking!'

'And we!' she said.

'And you!'

He wondered why she said nothing. Did she understand? He put his hand on her arm.

'Valentia!'

He had never called her by her Christian name before. She turned her face towards him.

'What do you mean?'

'Oh, Valentia, I love you! I can't help it.'

A sob burst from her.

'Didn't you understand,' he said, 'all those hours that I sat for you while you painted, and these long nights in which we wandered by the water?'

'I thought you were my friend.'

'I thought so too. When I sat before you and watched you paint, and looked at your beautiful hair and your eyes, I thought I was your friend. And I looked at the lines of your body beneath your dress. And when it pleased me to carry your easel and walk with you, I thought it was friendship. Only to-night I know I am in love. Oh, Valentia, I am so glad!'

She could not keep back her tears. Her bosom heaved, and she wept.

'You are a woman,' he said. 'Did you not see?'

'I am so sorry,' she said, her voice all broken. 'I thought we were such good friends. I was so happy. And now you have spoilt it all.'

'Valentia, I love you.'

'I thought our friendship was so good and pure. And I felt so strong in it. It seemed to me so beautiful.'

'Did you think I was less a man than the fisherman you see walking beneath the trees at night?'

'It is all over now,' she sighed.

'What do you mean?'

'I can't stay here with you alone.'

'You're not going away?'

'Before, there was no harm in our being together at the hotel; but now -'

'Oh, Valentia, don't leave me. I can't, I can't live without you.'

She heard the unhappiness in his voice. She turned to him again and laid her two hands on his shoulders.

'Why can't you forget it all, and let us be good friends again? Forget that you are a man. A woman can remain with a man forever, and always be content to walk and read and talk with him, and never think of anything else. Can you forget it, Ferdinand? You will make me so happy.'

He did not answer, and for a long time they stood on the bridge in silence. At last he sighed, a heartbroken sigh.

'Perhaps you're right. It may be better to pretend that we are friends. If you like, we will forget all this.'

Her heart was too full; she could not answer; but she held out her hands to him. He took them in his own, and, bending down, kissed them.

Then they walked home, side by side, without speaking.

V

Next morning Valentia received M. Rollo's answer to her letter. He apologised for his delay in answering.

'You are a philosopher,' he said, she could see the little snigger with which he had written the words, 'You are a philosopher, and I was afraid lest my reply should disturb the course of your reflections on friendship. I confess that I did not entirely understand your letter, but I gathered that the sentiments were correct, and it gave me great pleasure to know that your experiment has had such excellent results. I gather that you have not yet discovered that there is more than a verbal connection between Friendship and Love.'

The reference is to the French equivalents of those states of mind.

'But to speak seriously, dear child. You are young and beautiful now, but not so very many years shall pass before your lovely skin becomes coarse and muddy, and your teeth yellow, and the wrinkles appear about your mouth and eyes. You have not so very many years before you in which to collect sensations, and the recollection of one's loves is, perhaps, the greatest pleasure left to one's old age. To be virtuous, my dear, is admirable, but there are so many interpretations of virtue. For myself, I can say that I have never regretted the temptations to which I succumbed, but often the temptations I have resisted. Therefore, love, love, love! And remember that if love at sixty in a man is sometimes pathetic, in a woman at forty it is always ridiculous. Therefore, take your youth in both hands and say to yourself, "Life is short, but let me live before I die!"'

She did not show the letter to Ferdinand.

Next day it rained. Valentia retired to a room at the top of the house and began to paint, but the incessant patter on the roof got on her nerves; the painting bored her, and she threw aside the brushes in disgust. She came downstairs and found Ferdinand in the dining-room, standing at the window looking at the rain. It came down in one continual steady pour, and the water ran off the raised brickwork of the middle of the street to the gutters by the side, running along in a swift and murky rivulet. The red brick of the opposite house looked cold and cheerless in the wet.... He did not turn or speak to her as she came in. She remarked that it did not look like leaving off. He made no answer. She drew a chair to the second window and tried to read, but she could not understand what she was reading. And she looked out at the pouring rain and the red brick house opposite. She wondered why he had not answered.

The innkeeper brought them their luncheon. Ferdinand took no notice of the preparations.

'Will you come to luncheon, Mr White?' she said to him. 'It is quite ready.'

'I beg your pardon,' he said gravely, as he took his seat.

He looked at her quickly, and then immediately dropping his eyes, began eating. She wished he would not look so sad; she was very sorry for him.

She made an observation and he appeared to rouse himself. He replied and they began talking, very calmly and coldly, as if they had not known one another five minutes. They talked of Art with the biggest of A's, and they compared Dutch painting with Italian; they spoke of Rembrandt and his life.

'Rembrandt had passion,' said Ferdinand, bitterly, 'and therefore he was unhappy. It is only the sexless, passionless creature, the block of ice, that can be happy in this world.'

She blushed and did not answer.

The afternoon Valentia spent in her room, pretending to write letters, and she wondered whether Ferdinand was wishing her downstairs.

At dinner they sought refuge in abstractions. They talked of dykes and windmills and cigars, the history of Holland and its constitution, the constitution of the United States and the edifying spectacle of the politics of that blessed country. They talked of political economy and pessimism and cattle rearing, the state of agriculture in England, the foreign policy of the day, Anarchism, the President of the French Republic. They would have talked of bi-metallism if they could. People hearing them would have thought them very learned and extraordinarily staid.

At last they separated, and as she undressed Valentia told herself that Ferdinand had kept his promise. Everything was just as it had been before, and the only change was that he used her Christian name. And she rather liked him to call her Valentia.

But next day Ferdinand did not seem able to command himself. When Valentia addressed him, he answered in monosyllables, with eyes averted; but when she had her back turned, she felt that he was looking at her. After breakfast she went away painting haystacks, and was late for luncheon.

She apologised.

'It is of no consequence,' he said, keeping his eyes on the ground. And those were the only words he spoke to her during the remainder of the day. Once, when he was looking at her surreptitiously, and she suddenly turned round, their eyes met, and for a moment he gazed straight at her, then walked away. She wished he would not look so sad. As she was going to bed, she held out her hand to him to say good-night, and she added,

'I don't want to make you unhappy, Mr White. I'm very sorry.'

'It's not your fault,' he said. 'You can't help it, if you're a stock and a stone.'

He went away without taking the proffered hand. Valentia cried that night.

In the morning she found a note outside her door:

'Pardon me if I was rude, but I was not master of myself. I am going to Volendam; I hate Monnickendam.'

VI

Ferdinand arrived at Volendam. It was a fishing village, only three miles across country from Monnickendam, but the route, by steam tram and canal, was so circuitous, that, with luggage, it took one two hours to get from place to place. He had walked over there with Valentia, and it had almost tempted them to desert Monnickendam. Ferdinand took a room at the hotel and walked out, trying to distract himself. The village consisted of a couple of score of houses, built round a semi-circular dyke against the sea, and in the semi-circle lay the fleet of fishing boats. Men and women were sitting at their doors mending nets. He looked at the fishermen, great, sturdy fellows, with rough, weather-beaten faces, huge earrings dangling from their ears. He took note of their quaint costume, black stockings and breeches, the latter more baggy than a Turk's, and the crushed strawberry of their high jackets, cut close to the body. He remembered how he had looked at them with Valentia, and the group of boys and men that she had sketched. He remembered how they walked along, peeping into the houses, where everything was spick and span, as only a Dutch cottage can be, with old Delft plates hanging on the walls, and pots and pans of polished brass. And he looked over the sea to the island of Marken, with its masts crowded together, like a forest without leaf or branch. Coming to the end of the little town he saw the church of Monnickendam, the red steeple half-hidden by the trees. He wondered where Valentia was, what she was doing.

But he turned back resolutely, and, going to his room, opened his books and began reading. He rubbed his eyes and frowned, in order to fix his attention, but the book said nothing but Valentia. At last he threw it aside and took his Plato and his dictionary, commencing to translate a difficult passage, word for word. But whenever he looked up a word he could only see Valentia, and he could not make head or tail of the Greek. He threw it aside also, and set out walking. He walked as hard as he could away from Monnickendam.

The second day was not quite so difficult, and he read till his mind was dazed, and then he wrote letters home and told them he was enjoying himself tremendously, and he walked till he felt his legs dropping off.

Next morning it occurred to him that Valentia might have written. Trembling with excitement, he watched the postman coming down the street, but he had no letter for Ferdinand. There would be no more post that day.

But the next day Ferdinand felt sure there would be a letter for him; the postman passed by the hotel door without stopping. Ferdinand thought he should go mad. All day he walked up and down his room, thinking only of Valentia. Why did she not write?

The night fell and he could see from his window the moon shining over the clump of trees about Monnickendam church, he could stand it no longer. He put on his hat and walked across country; the three miles were endless; the church and the trees seemed to grow no nearer, and at last, when he thought himself close, he found he had a bay to walk round, and it appeared further away than ever.

He came to the mouth of the canal along which he and Valentia had so often walked. He looked about, but he could see no one. His heart beat as he approached the little bridge, but Valentia was not there. Of course she would not come out alone. He ran to the hotel and asked for her. They told him she was not in. He walked through the town; not a soul was to be seen. He came to the church; he walked round, and then, right at the edge of the trees, he saw a figure sitting on a bench.

She was dressed in the same flowered dress which she had worn when he likened her to a Dresden shepherdess; she was looking towards Volendam.

He went up to her silently. She sprang up with a little shriek.

'Ferdinand!'

'Oh, Valentia, I cannot help it. I could not remain away any longer. I could do nothing but think of you all day, all night. If you knew how I loved you! Oh, Valentia, have pity on me! I cannot be your friend. It's all nonsense about friendship; I hate it. I can only love you. I love you with all my heart and soul, Valentia.'

She was frightened.

'Oh! how can you stand there so coldly and watch my agony? Don't you see? How can you be so cold?'

'I am not cold, Ferdinand,' she said, trembling. 'Do you think I have been happy while you were away?'

'Valentia!'

'I thought of you, too, Ferdinand, all day, all night. And I longed for you to come back. I did not know till you went that, I loved you.'

'Oh, Valentia!'

He took her in his arms and pressed her passionately to him.

'No, for God's sake!'

She tore herself away. But again he took her in his arms, and this time he kissed her on the mouth. She tried to turn her face away.

'I shall kill myself, Ferdinand!'

'What do you mean?'

'In those long hours that I sat here looking towards you, I felt I loved you, I loved you as passionately as you said you loved me. But if you came back, and, anything happened, I swore that I would throw myself in the canal.'

He looked at her.

'I could not live afterwards,' she said hoarsely. 'It would be too horrible. I should be, oh, I can't think of it!'

He took her in his arms again and kissed her.

'Have mercy on me!' she cried.

'You love me, Valentia.'

'Oh, it is nothing to you. Afterwards you will be just the same as before. Why cannot men love peacefully like women? I should be so happy to remain always as we are now, and never change. I tell you I shall kill myself.'

'I will do as you do, Valentia.'

'You?'

'If anything happens, Valentia,' he said gravely, 'we will go down to the canal together.'

She was horrified at the idea; but it fascinated her.

'I should like to die in your arms,' she said.

For the second time he bent down and took her hands and kissed them. Then she went alone into the silent church, and prayed.

VII

They went home. Ferdinand was so pleased to be at the hotel again, near her. His bed seemed so comfortable; he was so happy, and he slept, dreaming of Valentia.

The following night they went for their walk, arm in arm; and they came to the canal. From the bridge they looked at the water. It was very dark; they could not hear it flow. No stars were reflected in it, and the trees by its side made the depth seem endless. Valentia shuddered. Perhaps in a little while their bodies would be lying deep down in the water. And they would be in one another's arms, and they would never be separated. Oh, what a price it was to pay! She looked tearfully at Ferdinand, but he was looking down at the darkness beneath them, and he was intensely grave.

And they wandered there by day and looked at the black reflection of the trees. And in the heat it seemed so cool and restful....

They abandoned their work. What did pictures and books matter now? They sauntered about the meadows, along shady roads; they watched the black and white cows sleepily browsing, sometimes coming to the water's edge to drink, and looking at themselves, amazed. They saw the huge-limbed milkmaids come along with their little stools and their pails, deftly tying the cow's hind legs that it might not kick. And the steaming milk frothed into the pails and was poured into huge barrels, and as each cow was freed, she shook herself a little and recommenced to browse.

And they loved their life as they had never loved it before.

One evening they went again to the canal and looked at the water, but they seemed to have lost their emotions before it. They were no longer afraid. Ferdinand sat on the parapet and Valentia leaned against him. He bent his head so that his face might touch her hair. She looked at him and smiled, and she almost lifted her lips. He kissed them.

'Do you love me, Ferdinand?'

He gave the answer without words.

Their faces were touching now, and he was holding her hands. They were both very happy.

'You know, Ferdinand,' she whispered, 'we are very foolish.'

'I don't care.'

'Monsieur Rollo said that folly was the chief attribute of man.'

'What did he say of love?'

'I forget.'

Then, after a pause, he whispered in her ear,

'I love you!'

And she held up her lips to him again.

'After all,' she said, 'we're only human beings. We can't help it. I think -'

She hesitated; what she was going to say had something of the anti-climax in it.

'I think, it would be very silly if, if we threw ourselves in the horrid canal.'

'Valentia, do you mean?'

She smiled charmingly as she answered,

'What you will, Ferdinand.'

Again he took both her hands, and, bending down, kissed them.... But this time she lifted him up to her and kissed him on the lips.

VIII

One night after dinner I told this story to my aunt.

'But why on earth didn't they get married?' she asked, when I had finished.

'Good Heavens!' I cried. 'It never occurred to me.'

'Well, I think they ought,' she said.

'Oh, I have no doubt they did. I expect they got on their bikes and rode off to the Consulate at Amsterdam there and then. I'm sure it would have been his first thought.'

'Of course, some girls are very queer,' said my aunt.

FAITH

I

The moon shone fitfully through the clouds on to the weary face of Brother Jasper kneeling in his cell. His hands were fervently clasped, uplifted to the crucifix that hung on the bare wall, and he was praying, praying as he had never prayed before. All through the hours of night, while the monks were sleeping, Brother Jasper had been supplicating his God for light; but in his soul remained a darkness deeper than that of the blackest night. At last he heard the tinkling of the bell that called the monks to prayers, and with a groan lifted himself up. He opened his cell door and went out into the cloister. With down-turned face he walked along till he came to the chapel, and, reaching his seat, sank again heavily to his knees.

The lights in the chapel were few enough, for San Lucido was nearly the poorest monastery in Spain; a few dim candles on the altar threw long shadows on the pavement, and in the choir their yellow glare lit up uncouthly the pale faces of the monks. When Brother Jasper stood up, the taper at his back cast an unnatural light over him, like a halo, making his great black eyes shine strangely from their deep sockets, while below them the dark lines and the black shadow of his shaven chin gave him an unearthly weirdness. He looked like a living corpse standing in the brown Franciscan cowl, a dead monk doomed for some sin to wander through the earth till the day, the Day of Judgment; and in the agony of that weary face one could almost read the terrors of eternal death.

The monks recited the service with their heavy drone, and the sound of the harsh men's voices ascended to the vault, dragging along the roof. But Jasper heard not what they said; he rose and knelt as they did; he uttered the words; he walked out of the church in his turn, and through the cloister to his cell. And he threw himself on the floor and beat his head against the hard stones, weeping passionately. And he cried out,

'What shall I do? What shall I do?'

For Brother Jasper did not believe.

II

Two days before, the monk, standing amid the stunted shrubs on the hill of San Lucido, had looked out on the arid plain before him. It was all brown and grey, the desolate ground strewn with huge granite boulders, treeless; and for the wretched sheep who fed there, thin and scanty grass; the shepherd, in his tattered cloak, sat on a rock, moodily, paying no heed to his flock, dully looking at the desert round him. Brother Jasper gazed at the scene as he had gazed for three years since he had come to San Lucido, filled with faith and great love for God. In those days he had thought nothing of the cold waste as his eyes rested on it; the light of heaven shed a wonderful glow on the scene, and when at sunset the heavy clouds were piled one above the other, like huge, fantastic mountains turned into golden fire, when he looked beyond them and saw the whole sky burning red and then a mass of yellow and gold, he could imagine that God was sitting there on His throne of fire, with Christ on His right hand in robes of light and glory, and Mary the Queen on His left. And above them the Dove with its outstretched wings, the white bird hovering in a sea of light! And it seemed so near! Brother Jasper felt in him almost the power to go there, to climb up those massy clouds of fire and attain the great joy, the joy of the presence of God.

The sun sank slowly, the red darkened into purple, and over the whole sky came a colour of indescribable softness, while in the east, very far away, shone out the star. And soon the soft faint blue sank before the night, and the stars in the sky were countless; but still in the west there was the shadow of the sun, a misty gleam. Over the rocky plain the heavens seemed so great, so high, that Brother Jasper sank down in his insignificance; yet he remembered the glories of the sunset, and felt that he was almost at the feet of God.

But now, when he looked at the clouds and the sun behind them, he saw no God; he saw the desert plain, the barrenness of the earth, the overladen, wretched donkey staggering under his pannier, and the broad-hatted peasant urging him on. He looked at the sunset and tried to imagine the Trinity that sat there, but he saw nothing. And he asked himself,

'Why should there be a God?'

He started up with a cry of terror, with his hands clasped to his head.

'My God! what have I done?'

He sank to his knees, humiliating himself. What vengeance would fall on him? He prayed passionately. But again the thought came; he shrieked with terror, he invoked the Mother of God to help him.

'Why should there be a God?'

He could not help it. The thought would not leave him that all this might exist without. How did he know? How could anyone be sure, quite sure? But he drove the thoughts away, and in his cell imposed upon himself a penance. It was Satan that stood whispering in his ear, Satan lying in wait for his soul; let him deny God and he would be damned forever.

He prayed with all his strength, he argued with himself, he cried out, 'I believe! I believe!' but in his soul was the doubt. The terror made him tremble like a leaf in the wind, and great drops of sweat stood on his forehead and ran heavily down his cheek. He beat his head against the wall, and in his agony swayed from side to side.... But he could not believe.

III

And for two days he had endured the torments of hell-fire, battling against himself in vain. The heavy lines beneath his eyes grew blacker than the night, his lips were pale with agony and fasting. He had not dared to speak to anyone, he could not tell them, and in him was the impulse to shout out, 'Why should there be?' Now he could bear it no longer. In the morning he went to the prior's cell, and, falling on his knees, buried his face in the old man's lap.

'Oh, father, help me! help me!'

The prior was old and wasted; for fifty years he had lived in the desert Castilian plain in the little monastery, all through his youth and manhood, through his age; and now he was older than anyone at San Lucido. White haired and wrinkled, but with a clear, rosy skin like a boy's; his soft blue eyes had shone with light, but a cataract had developed, and gradually his sight had left him till he could barely see the crucifix in his cell and the fingers of his hand; at last he could only see the light. But the prior did not lose the beautiful serenity of his life; he was always happy and kind; and feeling that his death could not now be very distant, he was filled with a heavenly joy that he would shortly see the face of God. Long hours he sat in his chair looking at the light with an indescribably charming smile hovering on his lips.

His voice broken by sobs, Brother Jasper told his story, while the prior gently stroked the young man's hands and face.

'Oh, father, make me believe!'

'One cannot force one's faith, my dear. It comes, it goes, and no man knows the wherefore. Faith does not come from reasoning; it comes from God.... Pray for it and rest in peace.'

'I want to believe so earnestly. I am so unhappy!'

'You are not the only one who has been tried, my son. Others have doubted before you and have been saved.'

'But if I died to-night, I should die in mortal sin.'

'Believe that God counts the attempt as worthy as the achievement.'

'Oh, pray for me, father, pray for me! I cannot stand alone. Give me your strength.'

'Go in peace, my son; I will pray for you, and God will give you strength!'

Jasper went away.

Day followed day, and week followed week; the spring came, and the summer; but there was no difference in the rocky desert of San Lucido. There were no trees to bud and burst into leaf, no flowers to bloom and fade; biting winds gave way to fiery heat, the sun beat down on the plain, and the sky was cloudless, cloudless, even the nights were so hot that the monks in their cells gasped for breath. And Brother Jasper brooded over the faith that was dead; and in his self-torment his cheeks became so hollow that the bones of his face seemed about to pierce the skin, the flesh shrunk from his hands, and the fingers became long and thin, like the claws of a vulture. He used to spend long hours with the prior, while the old man talked gently, trying to bring faith to the poor monk, that his soul might rest. But one day, in the midst of the speaking, the prior stopped, and Jasper saw an expression of pain pass over his face.

'What is it?'

'Nothing, my son,' he replied, smiling.... 'We enter the world with pain, and with pain we leave it!'

'What do you mean? Are you ill? Father! father!'

The prior opened his mouth and showed a great sloughing sore; he put Jasper's fingers to his neck and made him feel the enlarged and hardened glands.

'What is it? You must see a surgeon.'

'No surgeon can help me, Brother Jasper. It is cancer, the Crab, it is the way that God has sent to call me to Himself.'

Then the prior began to suffer the agonies of the disease, terrible pains shot through his head and neck; he could not swallow. It was a slow starvation; the torment kept him awake through night after night, and only occasionally his very exhaustion gave him a little relief so that he slept. Thinner and thinner he became, and his whole mouth was turned into a putrid, horrible sore. But yet he never murmured. Brother Jasper knelt by his bed, looking at him pitifully.

'How can you suffer it all? What have you done that God should give you this? Was it not enough that you were blind?'

'Ah, I saw such beautiful things after I became blind, all heaven appeared before me.'

'It is unjust, unjust!'

'My son, all is just.'

'You drive me mad!... Do you still believe in the merciful goodness of God?'

A beautiful smile broke through the pain on the old man's face.

'I still believe in the merciful goodness of God!'

There was a silence. Brother Jasper buried his face in his hands and thought brokenheartedly of his own affliction. How happy he could be if he had that faith.... But the silence in the room was more than the silence of people who did not speak. Jasper looked up suddenly.

The prior was dead.

Then the monk bent over the body and looked at the face into the opaque white eyes; there was no difference, the flesh was warm, everything was just the same, and yet ... and yet he was dead. What did they mean by saying the soul had fled? What had happened? Jasper understood nothing of it. And afterwards, before the funeral, when he looked at the corpse again, and it was cold and a horrible blackness stained the lips, he felt sure.

Brother Jasper could not believe in the resurrection of the dead. And the soul, what did they mean by the soul?

IV

Then a great loneliness came over him; the hours of his life seemed endless, and there was no one in whom he could find comfort. The prior had given him a ray of hope, but he was gone, and now Jasper was alone in the world.... And beyond? Oh! how could one be certain? It was awful this perpetual doubt, recurring more strongly than ever. Men had believed so long. Think of all the beautiful churches that had been made in the honour of God, and the pictures. Think of the works that had been done for his love, the martyrs who had cheerfully given up their lives. It seemed impossible that it should be all for nothing. But, but Jasper could not believe. And he cried out to the soul of the prior, resting in heaven, to come to him and help him. Surely, if he really were alive again, he would not let the poor monk whom he had loved linger in this terrible uncertainty. Jasper redoubled his prayers; for hours he remained on his knees, imploring God to send him light.... But no light came, and exhausted Brother Jasper sank into despair.

The new prior was a tall, gaunt man, with a great hooked nose and heavy lips; his keen, dark eyes shone fiercely from beneath his shaggy brows. He was still young, full of passionate energy. And with large gesture and loud, metallic voice he loved to speak of hell-fire and the pains of the damned, hating the Jews and heretics with a bitter personal hatred.

'To the stake!' he used to say. 'The earth must be purged of this vermin, and it must be purged by fire.'

He exacted the most absolute obedience from the monks, and pitiless was the punishment for any infringement of his rules.... Brother Jasper feared the man with an almost unearthly terror; when he felt resting upon him the piercing black eyes, he trembled in his seat, and a cold sweat broke out over him. If the prior knew, the thought almost made him faint. And yet the fear of it seemed to drag him on; like a bird before a serpent, he was fascinated. Sometimes he felt sudden impulses to tell him, but the vengeful eyes terrified him.

One day he was in the cloister, looking out at the little green plot in the middle where the monks were buried, wondering confusedly whether all that prayer and effort had been offered up to empty images of what, of the fear of Man? Turning round, he started back and his heart beat, for the prior was standing close by, looking at him with those horrible eyes. Brother Jasper trembled so that he could scarcely stand; he looked down.

'Brother Jasper!' The prior's voice seemed sterner than it had ever been before. 'Brother Jasper!'

'Father!'

'What have you to tell me?'

Jasper looked up at him; the blood fled from his lips.

'Nothing, my father!' The prior looked at him firmly, and Jasper thought he read the inmost secrets of his heart.

'Speak, Brother Jasper!' said the prior, and his voice was loud and menacing.

Then hurriedly, stuttering in his anxiety, the monk confessed his misery.... A horror came over the prior's face as he listened, and Jasper became so terrified that he could hardly speak; but the prior seemed to recover himself, and interrupted him with a furious burst of anger.

'You look over the plain and do not see God, and for that you doubt Him? Miserable fool!'

'Oh, father, have mercy on me! I have tried so hard. I want to believe. But I cannot.'

'I cannot! I cannot! What is that? Have men believed for a thousand years, has God performed miracle after miracle, and a miserable monk dares to deny Him?'

'I cannot believe!'

'You must!' His voice was so loud that it rang through the cloisters. He seized Jasper's clasped hands, raised in supplication before him, and forced him to his knees. 'I tell you, you shall believe!'

Quivering with wrath, he looked at the prostrate form at his feet, moved by convulsive weeping. He raised his hand as if to strike the monk, but with difficulty contained himself.

Then the prior bade Brother Jasper go to the church and wait. The monks were gathered together, all astonished. They stood in their usual places, but Jasper remained in the middle, away from them, with head cast down. The prior called out to them in his loud, clear voice,

'Pray, my brethren, pray for the soul of Brother Jasper, which lies in peril of eternal death.'

The monks looked at him suddenly, and Brother Jasper's head sank lower, so that no one could see his face. The prior sank to his knees and prayed with savage fervour. Afterwards the monks went their ways; but when Jasper passed them they looked down, and when by chance he addressed a novice, the youth hurried from him without answering. They looked upon him as accursed. The prior spoke no more, but often Jasper felt his stern gaze resting on him, and a shiver would pass through him. In the services Jasper stood apart from the rest, like an unclean thing; he did not join in their prayers, listening confusedly to their monotonous droning; and when a pause came and he felt all eyes turn to him, he put his hands to his face to hide himself.

'Pray, my brethren, pray for the soul of Brother Jasper, which lies in peril of eternal death.'

V

In his cell the monk would for days sit apathetically looking at the stone wall in front of him, sore of heart; the hours would pass by unnoticed, and only the ringing of the chapel bell awoke him from his stupor. And sometimes he would be seized with sudden passion and, throwing himself on his knees, pour forth a stream of eager, vehement prayer. He remembered the penances which the seraphic father imposed on his flesh, but he always had faith; and Jasper would scourge himself till he felt sick and faint, and, hoping to gain his soul by mortification of the body, refuse the bread and water which was thrust into his cell, and for a long while eat nothing. He became so weak and ill that he could hardly stand; and still no help came.

Then he took it into his head that God would pity him and send a miracle to drive away his uncertainty. Was he not anxious to believe, if only he could? so anxious! God would not send a miracle to a poor monk.... Yet miracles had been performed for smaller folk than he, for shepherds and tenders of swine. But Christ himself had said that miracles only came by faith, but Jasper remembered that often the profligate and the harlot had been brought to repentance by a vision. Even the Holy Francis had been but a loose gallant till Christ appeared to him. Yet, if Christ had appeared, it showed, ah! but how could one be sure? it might only have been a dream. Let a vision appear to him and he would believe. Oh, how enchanted he would be to believe, to rest in peace, to know that before him, however hard the life, were eternal joy and the kingdom of heaven.

But Brother Jasper put his hands to his head cruelly aching. He could not understand, he could not know, the doubt weighed on his brain like a sheet of lead; he felt inclined to tear his skull apart to relieve the insupportable pressure. How endless life was! Why could it not finish quickly and let him know? But supposing there really was a God, He would exact terrible vengeance. What punishment would He inflict on the monk who had denied Him, who had betrayed Him like a second Judas? Then a fantastic idea came into his crazy brain. Was it Satan that put all these doubts into his head? If it were, Satan must exist; and if he did, God existed too. He knew that the devil stood ready to appear to all who called. If Christ would not appear, let Satan show himself. It meant hell-fire; but if God were, the monk felt he was damned already, for the truth he would give his soul!

The idea sent a coldness through him, so that he shivered; but it possessed him, and he exulted, thinking that he would know at last. He rose from his bed, it was the dead of night and all the monks were sleeping and, trembling with cold, began to draw with chalk strange figures on the floor. He had seen them long ago in an old book of magic, and their fantastic shapes, fascinating him, had remained in his memory.

In the centre of the strange confusion of triangles he stood and uttered in a husky voice the invocation. He murmured uncouth words in an unknown language, and bade Satan stand forth.... He expected a thunderclap, the flashing of lightning, sulphurous fumes, but the night remained silent and quiet; not a sound broke the stillness of the monastery; the snow outside fell steadily.

VI

Next day the prior sent for him and repeated his solemn question.

'Brother Jasper, what have you to say to me?'

And absolutely despairing, Jasper answered,

'Nothing, nothing, nothing!'

Then the prior strode up to him in wrath and smote him on the cheek.

'It is a devil within you, a devil of obstinacy and pride. You shall believe!'

He cried to monks to lay hold of him; they dragged him roughly to the cloisters, and stripping him of his cowl tied it round his waist, and bound him by the hands to a pillar.... And the prior ordered them to give Jasper eight-and-thirty strokes with the scourge, one less than Christ, that the devil might be driven out. The scourge was heavy and knotted, and the porter bared his arms that he might strike the better; the monks stood round in eager expectation. The scourge whizzed through the air and came down with a thud on Jasper's bare shoulders; a tremor passed through him, but he did not speak. Again it came down, and as the porter raised it for the third time the monks saw great bleeding weals on Brother Jasper's back. Then, as the scourge fell heavily, a terrible groan burst from him. The porter swung his arm, and this time a shriek broke from the wretched monk; the blows came pitilessly and Jasper lost all courage. He shrieked with agony, imploring them to stop.

But ferociously the prior cried,

'Did Christ bear in silence forty stripes save one, and do you cry out like a woman before you have had ten!'

The porter went on, and the prior's words were interrupted by piercing shrieks.

'It is the devil crying out within him,' said the monks, gloating on the bleeding back and the face of agony.

Heavy drops of sweat ran off the porter's face and his arm began to tire; but he seized the handle with both hands and swung the knotted ropes with all his strength.

Jasper fainted.

'See!' said the prior. 'See the fate of him who has not faith in God!'

The cords with which he was tied prevented the monk from falling, and stroke after stroke fell on his back till the number was completed. Then they loosed him from the column, and he sank senseless and bleeding to the ground. They left him. Brother Jasper regained slowly his senses, lying out in the cold cloister with the snow on the graves in the middle; his hands and feet were stiff and blue. He shivered and drew himself together for warmth, then a groan burst from him, feeling the wounds of his back. Painfully he lifted himself up and crawled to the chapel door; he pushed it open, and, staggering forward, fell on his face, looking towards the altar. He remained there long, dazed and weary, pulling his cowl close round him to keep out the bitter cold. The pain of his body almost relieved the pain of his mind; he wished dumbly that he could lie there and die, and be finished with it all. He did not know the time; he wondered whether any service would soon bring the monks to disturb him. He took sad pleasure in the solitude, and in the great church the solitude seemed more intense. Oh, and he hated the monks! it was cruel, cruel, cruel! He put his hands to his face and sobbed bitterly.

But suddenly a warmth fell on him; he looked up, and the glow seemed to come from the crucified Christ in the great painted window by the altar. The monk started up with a cry and looked eagerly; the bell began to ring. The green colour of death was becoming richer, the glass gained the fulness of real flesh; now it was a soft round whiteness. And Brother Jasper cried out in ecstasy,

'It is Christ!'

Then the glow deepened, and from the Crucified One was shed a wonderful light like the rising of the sun behind the mountains, and the church was filled with its rich effulgence.

'Oh, God, it is moving!'

The Christ seemed to look at Brother Jasper and bow His head.

Two by two the monks walked silently in, and Brother Jasper lifted up his arms, crying:

'Behold a miracle! Christ has appeared to me!'

A murmur of astonishment broke from them, and they looked at Jasper gazing in ecstasy at the painted window.

'Christ has appeared to me…. I am saved!'

Then the prior came up to him and took him in his arms and kissed him.

'My son, praise be to God! you are whole again.'

But Jasper pushed him aside, so that he might not be robbed of the sight which filled him with rapture; the monks crowded round, questioning, but he took no notice of them. He stood with outstretched arms, looking eagerly, his face lighted up with joy. The monks began to kiss his cowl and his feet, and they touched his hands.

'I am saved! I am saved!'

And the prior cried to them,

'Praise God, my brethren, praise God! for we have saved the soul of Brother Jasper from eternal death.'

But when the service was over and the monks had filed out, Brother Jasper came to himself and he saw that the light had gone from the window; the Christ was cold and dead, a thing of the handicraft of man. What was it that had happened? Had a miracle occurred? The question flashing through his mind made him cry out. He had prayed for a miracle, and a miracle had been shown him, the poor monk of San Lucido….And now he doubted the miracle. Oh, God must have ordained the damnation of his soul to give him so little strength, perhaps He had sent the miracle that he might have no answer at the Day of Judgment.

'Faith thou hadst not, I showed Myself to thee in flesh and blood, I moved My head; thou didst not believe thine own eyes.' …

VII

Next day, at vespers, Jasper anxiously fixed his gaze on the stained-glass window, again a glow came from it, and as he moved the head seemed to incline itself; but now Jasper saw it was only the sun shining through the window, only the sun! Then the heaviness descended into the deepest parts of Jasper's soul, and he despaired.

The night came and Jasper returned to his cell.... He leant against the door, looking out through the little window, but he could only see the darkness. And he likened it to the darkness in his own soul.

'What shall I do?' he groaned.

He could not tell the monks that it was not a miracle he had seen; he could not tell them that he had lost faith again.... And then his thoughts wandering to the future,

'Must I remain all my life in this cold monastery? If there is no God, if I have but one life, what is the good of it? Why cannot I enjoy my short existence as other men? Am not I young, am not I of the same flesh and blood as they?'

Vague recollections came to him of those new lands beyond the ocean, those lands of sunshine and sweet odours. His mind became filled with a vision of broad rivers, running slow and cool, overshadowed by strange, luxuriant trees. And all was a wealth of beautiful colour.

'Oh, I cannot stay!' he cried; 'I cannot stay!'

And it was a land of loving-kindness, a land of soft-eyed, gentle women.

'I cannot stay! I cannot stay!'

The desire to go forth was overwhelming, the walls of his cell seemed drawing together to crush him; he must be free. Oh, for life! life! He started up, not seeing the madness of his adventure; he did not think of the snow-covered desert, the night, the distance from a town. He saw before him the glorious sunshine of a new life, and he went towards it like a blind man, with outstretched arms.

Everyone was asleep in the monastery. He crept out of his cell and silently opened the door of the porter's lodge; the porter was sleeping heavily. Jasper took the keys and unlocked the gate. He was free. He took no notice of the keen wind blowing across the desert; he hurried down the hill, slipping on the frozen snow.... Suddenly he stopped; he had caught sight of the great crucifix which stood by the wayside at the bottom of the hill. Then the madness of it all occurred to him. Wherever he went he would find the crucifix, even beyond the sea, and nowhere would he be able to forget his God. Always the recollection, always the doubt, and he would never have rest till he was in the grave. He went close to it and looked up; it was one of those strange Spanish crucifixes, a wooden image with long, thin arms and legs and protruding ribs, with real hair hanging over the shoulders, and a true crown of thorns placed on the head; the ends of the tattered cloth fastened about the loins fluttered in the wind. In the night the lifelikeness was almost ghastly; it might have been a real man that hung there, with great nails through his feet. The common people paid superstitious reverence to it, and Jasper had often heard the peasants tell of the consolations they had received.

Why should not he too receive consolation? Was his soul not as worth saving as theirs? A last spark of hope filled him, and he lifted himself up on tip-toe to touch the feet.

'Oh, Christ, come down to me! tell me whether Thou art indeed a God. Oh, Christ, help me!'

But the words lost themselves in the wind and night.... Then a great rage seized him that he alone should receive no comfort. He clenched his fists and beat passionately against the cross.

'Oh, you are a cruel God! I hate you, I hate you!'

If he could have reached it he would have torn the image down, and beat it as he had been beaten. In his impotent rage he shrieked out curses upon it, he blasphemed.

But his strength spent itself and he sank to the foot of the cross, bursting into tears. In his self-pity he thought his heart was broken. Lifting himself to his knees, he clasped the wood with his hands and looked up for the last time at the dead face of Christ.

It was the end.... A strange peace came over him as the anguish of his mind fell away before the cold. His hands and his feet were senseless, he felt his heart turning to ice, and he felt nothing.

In a little while the snow began to fall, lightly covering his shoulders. Brother Jasper knew the secret of death at last.

VIII

The day broke slowly, dim and grey. There was a hurried knocking at the porter's door, a peasant with white and startled face said that a brother was kneeling at the great cross in the snow, and would not speak.

The monks sallied forth anxiously, and came to the silent figure, clasping the cross in supplication.

'Brother Jasper!'

The prior touched his hands; they were as cold as ice.

'He is dead!'

The villagers crowded round in astonishment, whispering to one another. The monks tried to move him, but his hands, frozen to the cross, prevented them.

'He died in prayer, he was a saint!'

But a woman with a paralysed arm came near him, and in her curiosity touched his ragged cowl.... Suddenly she felt a warmth pass through her, and the dead arm began to tingle. She cried out in astonishment, and as the people turned to look she moved the fingers.

'He has restored my arm,' she said. 'Look!'

'A miracle!' they cried out. 'A miracle! He is a saint!'

The news spread like fire; and soon they brought a youth lying on a bed, wasted by a mysterious illness, so thin that the bones protruding had formed angry sores on the skin. They touched him with the hem of the monk's garment, and immediately he roused himself.

'I am whole; give me to eat!'

A murmur of wonder passed through the crowd. The monks sank to their knees and prayed.

At last they lifted up the dead monk and bore him to the church. But people all round the country crowded to see him; the sick and the paralysed came from afar, and often went away sound as when they were born.

They buried him at last, but still to his tomb they came from all sides, rich and poor; and the wretched monk, who had not faith to cure the disease of his own mind, cured the diseases of those who had faith in him.

THE CHOICE OF AMYNTAS

I

Often enough the lover of cities tires of their unceasing noise; the din of the traffic buzzes perpetually in his ears, and even in the silences of night he hears the footfalls on the pavement, the dull stamping of horses, the screeching of wheels; the fog chokes up the lungs so that he cannot breathe; he sees no longer any charms in the tall chimneys of the factory and the heavy smoke winding in curves against the leaden sky; then he flies to countries where the greenness is like cold spring water, where he can hear the budding of the trees and the stars tell him fantastic things, the silence is full of mysterious new emotions. And so the writer sometimes grows weary to death of the life he sees, and he presses his hands before his eyes, that he may hide from him the endless failure in the endless quest; then he too sets sail for Bohemia by the Sea, and the other countries of the Frankly Impossible, where men are always brave and women ever beautiful; there the tears of the morning are followed by laughter at night, trials are easily surmountable, virtue is always triumphant; there no illusions are lost, and lovers live ever happily in a world without end.

II

Once upon a time, very long ago, when the world was younger and more wicked than it is now, there lived in the West Country a man called Peter the Schoolmaster. But he was very different from ordinary schoolmasters, for he was a scholar and a man of letters; he was consequently very poor. All his life he had pored over old books and musty parchments; but from them he had acquired little wisdom, for one bright spring-time he fell in love with a farmer's daughter and married her. The farmer's daughter was a buxom wench, and, to the schoolmaster's delight, he had a careless, charming soul, she presented him in course of time with a round dozen of sturdy children. Peter compared himself with Priam of Troy, with Jacob, with King Solomon of Israel and with Queen Anne of England. Peter wrote a Latin ode to each offspring in turn, which he recited to the assembled multitude when the midwife put into his arms for the first time the new arrival. There was great rejoicing over the birth of every one of the twelve children; but, as was most proper in a land of primogeniture, the chiefest joy was the first-born; and to him Peter wrote an Horatian ode, which was two stanzas longer than the longest Horace ever wrote. Peter vowed that no infant had ever been given the world's greeting in so magnificent a manner; certainly he had never himself surpassed that first essay. As he told the parson, to write twelve odes on paternity, twelve greetings to the new-born soul, is a severe tax even on the most fertile imagination.

But the object of all this eloquence was the cause of the first and only quarrel between the gentle schoolmaster and his spouse; for the learned man had dug out of one of his old books the name of Amyntas, and Amyntas he vowed should be the name of his son; so with that trisyllable he finished every stanza of his ode. His wife threw her head back, and, putting her hands on her hips, stood with arms akimbo; she said that never in all her born days had she heard of anyone being called by such a name, which was more fit for a heathen idol than for a plain, straightforward member of the church by law established. In its stead she suggested that the boy be called Peter, after his father, or John, after hers. The gentle schoolmaster was in the habit of giving way to his wife in all things, and it may be surmised that this was the reason why the pair had lived in happiest concord; but now he was firm! He said it was impossible to call the boy by any other name than Amyntas.

'The name is necessary to the metre of my ode,' he said. 'It is its very life. How can I finish my stanzas with Petrus or Johannes? I would sooner die.'

His wife did not think the ode mattered a rap. Peter turned pale with emotion; he could scarcely express himself.

'Every mother in England has had a child; children have been born since the days of Cain and Abel thicker than the sands of the sea. What is a child? But an ode, my ode! A child is but an ordinary product of man and woman, but a poem is a divine product of the Muses. My poem is sacred; it shall not be defiled by any Petrus or Johannes! Let my house fall about my head, let my household gods be scattered abroad, let the Fates with their serpent hair render desolate my hearth; but do not rob me of my verse. I would sooner lose the light of my eyes than the light of my verse! Ah! let me wander through the land like Homer, sightless, homeless; let me beg my bread from door to door, and I will sing the ode, the ode to Amyntas.' ...

He said all this with so much feeling that Mrs Peter began to cry, and, with her apron up to her eyes, said that she didn't want him to go blind; but even if he did, he should never want, for she would work herself to the bone to keep him. Peter waved his hand in tragic deprecation. No, he would beg his bread from door to door; he would sleep by the roadside in the bitter winter night.

Now, the parson was present during this colloquy, and he proposed an arrangement; and finally it was settled that Peter should have his way in this case, but that Mrs Peter should have the naming of all subsequent additions to the family. So, of the rest, one was called Peter, and one was called John, and there was a Mary, and a Jane, and a Sarah; but the eldest, according to agreement, was christened Amyntas, although to her dying day, notwithstanding the parson's assurances, the mother was convinced in her heart of hearts that the name was papistical and not fit for a plain, straightforward member of the church by law established.

III

Now, it was as clear as a pikestaff to Peter the Schoolmaster that a person called Amyntas could not go through the world like any other ordinary being; so he devoted particular care to his son's education, teaching him, which was the way of schoolmasters then as now, very many entirely useless things, and nothing that could be to him of the slightest service in earning his bread and butter.

But twelve children cannot be brought up on limpid air, and there were often difficulties when new boots were wanted; sometimes, indeed, there were difficulties when bread and meat and puddings were wanted. Such things did not affect Peter; he felt not the pangs of hunger as he read his books, and he vastly preferred to use the white and the yolk of an egg in the restoration of an old leather binding than to have it solemnly cooked and thrust into his belly. What cared he for the rantings of his wife and the crying of the children when he could wander in imagination on Mount Ida, clad only in his beauty, and the three goddesses came to him promising wonderful things? He was a tall, lean man, with thin, white hair and blue eyes, but his wrinkled cheeks were still rosy; incessant snuff-taking had given a special character to his nose. And sometimes, taking upon him the spirit of Catullus, he wrote verses to Lesbia, or, beneath the breast-plate of Marcus Aurelius, he felt his heart beat bravely as he marched against the barbarians; he was Launcelot, and he made charming speeches to Guinevere as he kissed her long white hand....

But now and then the clamour of the outer world became too strong, and he had to face seriously the question of his children's appetite.

It was on one of these occasions that the schoolmaster called his son to his study and said to him,

'Amyntas, you are now eighteen years of age. I have taught you all I know, and you have profited by my teaching; you know Greek and Latin as well as I do myself; you are well acquainted with Horace and Tully; you have read Homer and Aristotle; and added to this, you can read the Bible in the original Hebrew. That is to say, you have all knowledge at your fingers' ends, and you are prepared to go forth and conquer the world. Your mother will make a bundle of your clothes; I will give you my blessing and a guinea, and you can start to-morrow.'

Then he returned to his study of an oration of Isocrates. Amyntas was thunder-struck.

'But, father, where am I to go?'

The schoolmaster raised his head in surprise, looking at his son over the top of his spectacles.

'My son,' he said, with a wave of the arm; 'my son, you have the world before you, is that not enough?'

'Yes, father,' said Amyntas, who thought it was a great deal too much; 'but what am I to do? I can't get very far on a guinea.'

'Amyntas,' answered Peter, rising from his chair with great dignity, 'have you profited so ill by the examples of antiquity, which you have had placed before you from your earliest years? Do you not know that riches consist in an equal mind, and happiness in golden mediocrity? Did the wise Odysseus quail before the unknown, because he had only a guinea in his pocket? Shame on the heart that doubts! Leave me, my son, and make ready.'

Amyntas, very crestfallen, left the room and went to his mother to acquaint her with the occurrence. She was occupied in the performance of the family's toilet.

'Well, my boy,' she said, as she scrubbed the face of the last but one, 'it's about time that you set about doing something to earn your living, I must say. Now, if instead of learning all this popish stuff about Greek and Latin and Lord knows what, you'd learnt to milk a cow or groom a horse you'd be as right as a trivet now. Well, I'll put you up a few things in a bundle as your father says and you can start early to-morrow morning.... Now then, darling,' she added, turning to her Benjamin, 'come and have your face washed, there's a dear.'

IV

Amyntas scratched his head, and presently an inspiration came to him.

'I will go to the parson,' he said.

The parson had been hunting, and he was sitting in his study in a great oak chair, drinking a bottle of port; his huge body and his red face expressed the very completest satisfaction with the world in general; one felt that he would go to bed that night with the cheerful happiness of duty performed, and snore stentoriously for twelve hours. He was troubled by no qualms of conscience; the Thirty-nine Articles caused him never a doubt, and it had never occurred to him to concern himself with the condition of the working classes. He lived in a golden age, when the pauper was allowed to drink himself to death as well as the nobleman, and no clergyman's wife read tracts by his bedside....

Amyntas told his news.

'Well, my boy', he never spoke but he shouted, 'so you're going away? Well, God bless you!'

Amyntas looked at him expectantly, and the parson, wondering what he expected, came to the conclusion that it was a glass of port, for at that moment he was able to imagine nothing that man could desire more. He smiled benignly upon Amyntas, and poured him out a glass.

'Drink that, my boy. Keep it in your memory. It's the finest thing in the world. It's port that's made England what she is!'

Amyntas drank the port, but his face did not express due satisfaction.

'Damn the boy!' said the parson. 'Port's wasted on him.' ... Then, thinking again what Amyntas might want, he rose slowly from his chair, stretching his legs. 'I'm not so young as I used to be; I get stiff after a day's hunting.' He walked round his room, looking at his bookshelves; at last he picked out a book and blew the dust off the edges. 'Here's a Bible for you, Amyntas. The two finest things in the world are port and the Bible.'

Amyntas thanked him, but without great enthusiasm. Another idea struck the parson, and he shouted out another question.

'Have you any money?'

Amyntas told him of the guinea.

'Damn your father! What's the good of a guinea?' He went to a drawer and pulled out a handful of gold, the tithes had been paid a couple of days before. 'Here are ten; a man can go to hell on ten guineas.'

'Thank you very much, sir,' said Amyntas, pocketing the money, 'but I don't think I want to go quite so far just yet.'

'Then where the devil do you want to go?' shouted the parson.

'That's just what I came to ask you about.'

'Why didn't you say so at once? I thought you wanted a glass of port. I'd sooner give ten men advice than one man port.' He went to the door and called out, 'Jane, bring me another bottle.' He drank the bottle in silence, while Amyntas stood before him, resting now upon one leg now upon another, turning his cap round and round in his hands. At last the parson spoke.

'You may look upon a bottle of port in two ways,' he said; 'you may take it as a symbol of a happy life or as a method of thought.... There are four glasses in a bottle. The first glass is full of expectation; you enter life with mingled feelings; you cannot tell whether it will be good or no. The second glass has the full savour of the grape; it is youth with vine-leaves in its hair and the passion of young blood. The third glass is void of emotion; it is grave and calm, like middle age; drink it slowly, you are in full possession of yourself, and it will not come again. The fourth glass has the sadness of death and the bitter sweetness of retrospect.'

He paused a moment for Amyntas to weigh his words.

'But a bottle of port is a better method of thought than any taught by the school-men. The first glass is that of contemplation, I think of your case; the second is apprehension, an idea occurs to me; the third is elaboration, I examine the idea and weigh the pros and cons; the fourth is realisation, and here I give you the completed scheme. Look at this letter; it is from my old friend Van Tiefel, a Dutch merchant who lives at Cadiz, asking for an English clerk. One of his ships is sailing from Plymouth next Sunday, and it will put in at Cadiz on the way to Turkey.'

Amyntas thought the project could have been formed without a bottle of port, but he was too discreet to say so, and heartily thanked the parson. The good man lived in a time when teetotalism had not ruined the clergy's nerves, and sanctity was not considered incompatible with a good digestion and common humanity....

V

Amyntas spent the evening bidding tender farewells to a round dozen of village beauties, whose susceptible hearts had not been proof against the brown eyes and the dimples of the youth. There was indeed woe when he spread the news of his departure; and all those maiden eyes ran streams of salt tears as he bade them one by one good-bye; and though he squeezed their hands and kissed their lips, vowing them one and all the most unalterable fidelity, they were perfectly inconsolable. It is an interesting fact to notice that the instincts of the true hero are invariably polygamic....

It was lucky for Amyntas that the parson had given him money, for his father, though he gave him a copy of the Ethics of Aristotle and his blessing, forgot the guinea; and Amyntas was too fearful of another reproach to remind him of it.

Amyntas was up with the lark, and having eaten as largely as he could in his uncertainty of the future, made ready to start. The schoolmaster had retired to his study to conceal his agitation; he was sitting like Agamemnon with a dishcloth over his head, because he felt his face unable to express his emotion. But the boy's mother stood at the cottage door, wiping her eyes with the corner of her apron, surrounded by her weeping children. She threw her arms about her son's neck, giving him a loud kiss on either cheek, and Amyntas went the round of his brothers and sisters, kissing them and bidding them not forget him. To console them, he promised to bring back green parrots and golden bracelets, and embroidered satins from Japan. As he passed down the village street he shook hands with the good folk standing at their doors to bid him good-bye, and slowly made his way into the open country.

VI

The way of the hero is often very hard, and Amyntas felt as if he would choke as he walked slowly along. He looked back at every step, wondering when he would see the old home again. He loitered through the lanes, taking a last farewell of the nooks and corners where he had sat on summer evenings with some fair female friend, and he heartily wished that his name were James or John, and that he were an ordinary farmer's son who could earn his living without going out for it into the wide, wide world. So may Dick Whittington have meditated as he trudged the London road, but Amyntas had no talismanic cat and no church bells rang him inspiring messages. Besides, Dick Whittington had in him from his birth the makings of a Lord Mayor, he had the golden mediocrity which is the surest harbinger of success. But to Amyntas the world seemed cold and grey, notwithstanding the sunshine of the morning; and the bare branches of the oak trees were gnarled and twisted like the fingers of evil fate. At last he came to the top of a little hill whence one had the last view of the village. He looked at the red-roofed church nestling among the trees, and in front of the inn he could still see the sign of the 'Turk's Head.' A sob burst from him; he felt he could not leave it all; it would not be so bad if he could see it once more. He might go back at night and wander through the streets; he could stand outside his own home door and look up at his father's light, perhaps seeing his father's shadow bent over his books. He cared nothing that his name was Amyntas; he would go to the neighbouring farmers and offer his services as labourer, the village barber wanted an apprentice. Ah! he would ten times sooner be a village Hampden or a songless Milton than any hero! He hid his face in the grass and cried as if his heart were breaking.

Presently he cried himself to sleep, and when he awoke the sun was high in the heavens and he had the very healthiest of appetites. He repaired to a neighbouring inn and ordered bread and cheese and a pot of beer. Oh, mighty is the power of beer! Why am I not a poet, that I may stand with my hair dishevelled, one hand in my manly bosom and the other outstretched with splendid gesture, to proclaim the excellent beauty of beer? Avaunt! ye sallow teetotalers, ye manufacturers of lemonade, ye cocoa-drinkers! You only see the sodden wretch who hangs about the public-house door in filthy slums, blinking his eyes in the glaze of electric light, shivering in his scanty rags, and you do not know the squalor and the terrible despair of hunger which he strives to forget.... But above all, you do not know the glorious ale of the country, the golden brown ale, with its scent of green hops, its broad scents of the country; its foam is whiter than snow and lighter than the almond blossoms; and it is cold, cold.... Amyntas drank his beer, and he sighed with great content; the sun shone hopefully upon him now, and the birds twittered all sorts of inspiring things; still in his mouth was the delightful bitterness of the hops. He threw off care as a mantle, and he stepped forward with joyful heart. Spain was a wild country, the land of the grave hidalgo and the haughty princess. He felt in his strong right arm the power to fight and kill and conquer. Black-bearded villains should capture beautiful maidens on purpose for him to rescue. Van Tiefel was but a stepping-stone; he was not made for the desk of a counting-house. No heights dazzled him; he saw himself being made a peer or a prince, being granted wide domains by a grateful monarch. He was not too low to aspire to the hand of a king's fair daughter; he was a hero, every inch a hero. Great is the power of beer. Avaunt! ye sallow teetotalers, ye manufacturers of lemonade, ye cocoa-drinkers!

At night he slept on a haystack, with the blue sky, star-bespangled, for his only roof, and dreamed luxurious dreams.... The mile-stones flew past one another as he strode along, two days, three days, four days. On the fifth, as he reached the summit of a little hill, he saw a great expanse of light shining in the distance, and the sea glittered before him like the bellies of innumerable little silver fishes. He went down the hill, up another, and thence saw Plymouth at his feet; the masts of the ships were like a great forest of leafless trees.... He thanked his stars, for one's imagination is all very well for a while, and the thought of one's future prowess certainly shortens the time; but roads are hard and hills are steep, one's legs grow tired and one's feet grow sore; and things are not so rose-coloured at the end of a journey as at the beginning. Amyntas could not for ever keep thinking of beautiful princesses and feats of arms, and after the second day he had exhausted every possible adventure; he had raised himself to the highest possible altitudes, and his aristocratic amours had had the most successful outcome.

He sat down by a little stream that ran along the roadside, and bathed his aching feet; he washed his face and hands; starting down the hill, he made his way towards the town and entered the gate.

VII

Amyntas discovered Captain Thorman of the good ship Calderon drinking rum punch in a tavern parlour. In those days all men were heroic.... He gave him the parson's letter.

'Well, my boy,' said the captain, after twice reading it; 'I don't mind taking you to Cadiz; I daresay you'll be able to make yourself useful on board. What can you do?'

'Please, sir,' answered Amyntas, with some pride, 'I know Latin and Greek; I am well acquainted with Horace and Tully; I have read Homer and Aristotle; and added to this, I can read the Bible in the original Hebrew.'

The captain looked at him.

'If you talk to me like that,' he said, 'I'll shy my glass at your head.' He shook with rage, and the redness of his nose emitted lightning sparks of indignation; when he had recovered his speech, he asked Amyntas why he stood there like an owl, and told him to get on board.

Amyntas bowed himself meekly out of the room, went down to the harbour, and bearing in mind what he had heard of the extreme wickedness of Plymouth, held tightly on to his money; he had been especially warned against the women who lure the unwary seaman into dark dens and rob him of money and life. But no adventure befell him, thanks chiefly to the swiftness of his heels, for when a young lady of prepossessing appearance came up to him and inquired after his health, affectionately putting her arm in his, he promptly took to his legs and fled.

Amyntas was in luck's way, for it was not often that an English ship carried merchandise to Spain. As a rule, the two powers were at daggers drawn; but at this period they had just ceased cutting one another's throats and sinking one another's ships, joining together in fraternal alliance to cut the throats and sink the ships of a rival power, which, till the treaty, had been a faithful and brotherly ally to His Majesty of Great Britain, and which our gracious king had abandoned with unusual dexterity, just as it was preparing to abandon him....

As Amyntas stood on the deck of the ship and saw the grey cliffs of Albion disappear into the sea, he felt the emotions and sentiments which inevitably come to the patriotic Englishman who leaves his native shore; his melancholy became almost unbearable as the ship, getting out into the open sea, began to roll, and he drank to the dregs the bitter cup of leaving England, home, beauty, and terra firma. He went below, and, climbing painfully into his hammock, gave himself over to misery and mal-de-mer.

Two days he spent of lamentation and gnashing of teeth, wishing he had never been born, and not till the third day did he come on deck. He was pale and weak, feeling ever so unheroic, but the sky was blue and the ship bounded over the blue waves as if it were alive. Amyntas sniffed in the salt air and the rushing wind, and felt alive again. The days went by, the sun became hotter, and the sky a different, deeper blue, while its vault spread itself over the sea in a vaster expanse. They came in sight of land again; they coasted down a gloomy country with lofty cliffs going sheer into the sea; they passed magnificent galleons laden with gold from America; and one morning, when Amyntas came on deck at break of day, he saw before him the white walls and red roofs of a southern city. The ship slowly entered the harbour of Cadiz.

VIII

At last! Amyntas went on shore immediately. His spirit was so airy within him that he felt he could hover along in the air, like Mr Lang's spiritualistic butlers, and it was only by a serious effort of will that he walked soberly down the streets like normal persons. His soul shouted with the joy of living. He took in long breaths as if to breathe in the novelty and the strangeness. He walked along, too excited to look at things, only conscious of a glare of light and colour, a thronging crowd, life and joyousness on every side.... He walked through street after street, almost sobbing with delight, through narrow alleys down which the sun never fell, into big squares hot as ovens and dazzling, uphill and downhill, past ragged slums, past the splendid palaces of the rich, past shops, past taverns. Finally he came on to the shore again and threw himself down in the shade of a little grove of orange trees to sleep.

When he awoke, he saw, standing motionless by his side, a Spanish lady. He looked at her silently, noting her olive skin, her dark and lustrous eyes, the luxuriance of her hair. If she had only possessed a tambourine she would have been the complete realisation of his dreams. He smiled.

'Why do you lie here alone, sweet youth?' she asked, with an answering smile. 'And who and what are you?'

'I lay down here to rest, lady,' he replied. 'I have this day arrived from England, and I am going to Van Tiefel, the merchant.'

'Ah! a young English merchant. They are all very rich. Are you?'

'Yes, lady,' frankly answered Amyntas, pulling out his handful of gold.

The Spaniard smiled on him, and then sighed deeply.

'Why do you sigh?' he asked.

'Ah! you English merchants are so fascinating.' She took his hand and pressed it. Amyntas was not a forward youth, but he had some experience of English maidens, and felt that there was but one appropriate rejoinder. He kissed her.

She sighed again as she relinquished herself to his embrace.

'You English merchants are so fascinating, and so rich.'

Amyntas thought the Spanish lady was sent him by the gods, for she took him to her house and gave him melons and grapes, which, being young and of lusty appetite, he devoured with great content. She gave him wine, strong, red, fiery wine, that burned his throat, and she gave him sundry other very delightful things, which it does not seem necessary to relate.

When Amyntas on his departure shyly offered some remuneration for his entertainment, it was with an exquisite southern grace that she relieved him of his ten golden guineas, and he almost felt she was doing him a favour as she carelessly rattled the coins into a silken purse. And if he was a little dismayed to see his treasure go so speedily, he was far too delicate-minded to betray any emotion; but he resolved to lose no time in finding out the offices of the wealthy Tiefel.

IX

But Van Tiefel was no longer in Cadiz! On the outbreak of the treaty, the Spanish authorities had given the Dutch merchant four-and-twenty hours to leave the country, and had seized his property, making him understand that it was only by a signal mercy that his life was spared. Amyntas rushed down to the harbour in dismay. The good ship Calderon had already sailed. Amyntas cursed his luck, he cursed himself; above all, he cursed the lovely Spanish lady whose charms had caused him to delay his search for Van Tiefel till the ship had gone on its eastward journey.

After looking long and wistfully at the sea, he turned back into the town and rambled melancholy through the streets, wondering what would become of him. Soon the pangs of hunger assailed him, and he knew the discomfort of a healthy English appetite. He hadn't a single farthing, and even Scotch poets, when they come to London to set the Thames on fire, are wont to put a half-crown piece in their pockets. Amyntas meditated upon the folly of extravagance, the indiscretion of youth and the wickedness of woman.... He tightened his belt and walked on. At last, feeling weary and faint with hunger, he lay down on the steps of a church and there spent the night. When he awoke next morning, he soon remembered that he had slept supperless; he was ravenous. Suddenly his eye, looking across the square, caught sight of a book shop, and it occurred to him that he might turn to account the books which his father and the parson had given him. He blessed their foresight. The Bible fetched nothing, but the Aristotle brought him enough to keep him from starvation for a week. Having satisfied his hunger, he set about trying to find work. He went to booksellers and told them his accomplishments, but no one could see any use in a knowledge of Greek, Latin and the Hebrew Bible. He applied at shops. Growing bolder with necessity, he went into merchants' offices, and to great men's porters, but all with great civility sent him about his business, and poor Amyntas was no more able to get work than nowadays a professional tramp or the secretary of a trade's union.

Four days he went on, trying here and trying there, eating figs and melons and bread, drinking water, sleeping beneath archways or on the steps of churches, and he dreamed of the home of roast beef and ale which he had left behind him. Every day he became more disheartened. But at last he rose up against Fate; he cursed it Byronically. Every man's hand was against him; his hand should be against every man. He would be a brigand! He shook off his feet the dust of Cadiz, and boldly went into the country to find a band of free companions. He stopped herdsmen and pedlars and asked them where brigands were. They pointed to the mountains, and to the mountains he turned his face. He would join the band, provoke a quarrel with the chief, kill him and be made chief in his stead. Then he would scour the country in a velvet mask and a peaked hat with a feather in it, carrying fire and desolation everywhere. A price would be set on his head, but he would snap his fingers in the face of the Prime Minister. He would rule his followers with an iron hand. But now he was in the midst of the mountains, and there were not the smallest signs of lawless folk, not even a gibbet with a skeleton hanging in chains to show where lawless folk had been. He sought high and low, but he never saw a living soul besides a few shepherds clothed in skins. It was most disheartening! Once he saw two men crouching behind a rock, and approached them; but as soon as they saw him they ran away, and although he followed them, shouting that they were not to be afraid since he wanted to be a brigand too, they paid no attention, but only ran the faster, and at last he had to give up the chase for want of breath. One can't be a robber chief all by oneself, nor is it given to everyone in this world to be a brigand. Amyntas found that even heroes have their limitations.

X

One day, making his way along a rocky path, he found a swineherd guarding his flock.

'Good-morrow!' said the man, and asked Amyntas whither he was bound.

'God knows!' answered Amyntas. 'I am wandering at chance, and know not where I go.'

'Well, youth, stay the night with me, and to-morrow you can set out again. In return for your company I will give you food and shelter.'

Amyntas accepted gratefully, for he had been feeding on herbs for a week, and the prospect of goat's milk, cheese and black bread was like the feast of Trimalchion. When Amyntas had said his story, the herdsman told him that there was a rich man in the neighbouring village who wanted a swineherd, and in the morning showed him the way to the rich man's house.

'I will come a little way with you lest you take the wrong path.' ...

They walked along the rocky track, and presently the way divided.

'This path to the right leads to the village,' said the man.

'And this one to the left, swineherd?'

The swineherd crossed himself.

'Ah! that is the path of evil fortune. It leads to the accursed cavern.'

A cold wind blew across their faces.

'Come away,' said the herdsman, shuddering. 'Do you not feel on your face the cold breath of it?'

'Tell me what it is,' said Amyntas. He stood looking at the opening between the low trees.

'It is a lake of death, a lake beneath the mountain, and the roof of it is held up by marble columns, which were never wrought by the hand of man. Come away! do you not feel on your face the cold breath of it?'

He dragged Amyntas away along the path that led to the village, and when the way was clear before him, turned back, returning to his swine. But Amyntas ran after him.

'Tell me what they say of the accursed cavern.'

'They say many things. Some say it is a treasure-house of the Moors, where they have left their wealth. Some say it is an entrance to the enchanted land; some say it is an entrance to hell itself.... Venturous men have gone in to discover the terrible secret, but none has returned to tell it.'

Amyntas wandered slowly towards the village. Were his dreams to end in the herding of swine? What was this cavern of which the herdsman spoke? He felt a strange impulse to go back and look at the dark opening between the little trees from which blew the cold wind.... But perhaps the rich man had a beauteous daughter; history is full of the social successes of swine herds. Amyntas felt a strange thrill as the dark lake came before his mind; he almost heard the lapping of the water.... Kings' daughters had often looked upon lowly swineherds and raised them to golden thrones. But he could not help going to look again at the dark opening between the little trees. He walked back and again the cold breath blew against his face; he felt in it the icy coldness of the water. It drew him in; he separated the little trees on either side. He walked on as if a hidden power urged him. And now the path became less clear; trees and bushes grew in the way and hindered him, brambles and long creeping plants twisted about his legs and pulled him back. But the wind with its coldness of the black water drew him on.... The birds of the air were hushed, and not one of the thousand insects of the wood uttered a note. Great trees above him hid the light. The silence was ghastly; he felt as if he were the only person in the world.

Suddenly he gave a cry; he had come to the end of the forest, and before him he saw the opening of the cavern. He looked in; he saw black, stagnant water, motionless and heavy, and, as far as the eye could reach, sombre pillars, covered with green, moist slime; they stood half out of the water, supporting the roof, and from the roof oozed moisture which fell in heavy drops, in heavy drops continually. At the entrance was a little skiff with a paddle in it.

Amyntas stood at the edge. Dared he venture? What could there be behind that darkness? The darkness was blacker than the blackest night. He stepped into the boat. Should he go? With beating heart he untied the rope; he hardly dared to breathe. He pushed away.

He looked to the right and left, paddling slowly; on all sides he saw the slimy columns stretching regularly into the darkness. The light of the open day grew dimmer as he advanced, the air became colder. He looked eagerly around him, paddling slowly. Already he half repented the attempt. The boat went along easily, and the black and heavy water hardly splashed as he drew his paddle through it. Still nothing could be seen but the even ranks of pillars. Then, all at once, the night grew blacker, and again the cold wind arose and blew in his face; everywhere was the ghastly silence and the darkness. A shiver went through him; he could not bear it; in an agony of terror he turned his paddle to go back. Whatever might be the secret of the cavern or the reward of the adventure, he dared go no further. He must get back quickly to the open air and the blue sky. He drew his paddle through the water. The boat did not turn. He gave a cry, he pulled with all his might, the boat only lurched a little and went on its way. He set his teeth and backed; his life depended upon it. The boat swam on. A cold sweat broke out over him; he put all his strength in his stroke. The boat went on into the darkness swiftly and silently. He paused a little to regain force; he stifled a sob of horror and despair. Then he made a last effort; the skiff whirled round into another avenue of columns, and the paddle shivered into atoms against a pillar. The little light of the cavern entrance was lost, and there was utter darkness.

Amyntas cowered down in the boat. He gave up hope of life, and lay there for long hours awaiting his end; the water carried the skiff along swiftly, silently. The darkness was so heavy that the columns were invisible, heavy drops fell into the water from the roof. How long would it last? Would the boat go on till he died, and then speed on forever? He thought of the others who had gone into the cavern. Were there other boats hurrying eternally along the heavy waters, bearing cold skeletons?

He covered his face with his hands and moaned. But he started up, the night seemed less black; he looked intently; yes, he could distinguish the outlines of the pillars dimly, so dimly that he thought he saw them only in imagination. And soon he could see distinctly their massive shapes against the surrounding darkness. And as gradually the night thinned away into dim twilight, he saw that the columns were different from those at the entrance of the cavern; they were no longer covered with weed and slime, the marble was polished and smooth; and the water beneath him appeared less black. The skiff went on so swiftly that the perpetual sequence of the pillars tired his eyes; but their grim severity gave way to round columns less forbidding and more graceful; as the light grew clearer, there was almost a tinge of blue in the water. Amyntas was filled with wonder, for the columns became lighter and more decorated, surmounted by capitals, adorned with strange sculptures. Some were green and some were red, others were yellow or glistening white; they mirrored themselves in the sapphire water. Gradually the roof raised itself and the columns became more slender; from them sprang lofty arches, gorgeously ornamented, and all was gold and silver and rich colour. The water turned to a dazzling, translucent blue, so that Amyntas could see hundreds of feet down to the bottom, and the bottom was covered with golden sand. And the light grew and grew till it was more brilliant than the clearest day; gradually the skiff slowed down and it swam leisurely towards the light's source, threading its way beneath the horse-shoe arches among the columns, and these gathered themselves into two lines to form a huge avenue surmounted by a vast span, and at the end, in a splendour of light, Amyntas saw a wondrous palace, with steps leading down to the water. The boat glided towards it and at the steps ceased moving.

At the same moment the silver doors of the palace were opened, and from them issued black slaves, magnificently apparelled; they descended to Amyntas and with courteous gestures assisted him out of the boat. Then two other slaves, even more splendidly attired than their fellows, came down and led Amyntas slowly and with great state into the court of the palace, at the end of which was a great chamber; into this they motioned the youth to enter. They made him the lowest possible bows and retired, letting a curtain fall over the doorway. But immediately the curtain was raised and other slaves came in, bearing gorgeous robes and all kinds of necessaries for the toilet. With much ceremony they proceeded to bathe and scent the fortunate creature; they polished and dyed his finger nails; they pencilled his eyebrows and faintly darkened his long eyelashes; they put precious balsam on his hair; then they clothed him in silken robes glittering with gold and silver; they put the daintiest red morocco shoes on his feet, a jewelled chain about his neck, rings on his fingers, and in his turban a rich diamond. Finally they placed before him a gigantic mirror, and left him.

Everything had been conducted in complete silence, and Amyntas throughout had preserved the most intense gravity. But when he was alone he gave a little silent laugh of delight. It was obvious that at last he was to be rewarded according to his deserts. He looked at the rings on his fingers, resisting a desire to put one or two of them in his pocket in case of a future rainy day. Then, catching sight of himself in the mirror, he started. Was that really himself? How very delightful! He made sure that no one could see, and then began to make bows to himself in the mirror; he walked up and down the room, observing the stateliness of his gesture; he waved his hands in a lordly and patronising fashion; he turned himself round to look at his back; he was very annoyed that he could not see his profile. He came to the conclusion that he looked every inch a king's son, and his inner consciousness told him that consequently the king's daughter could not be far off.

But he would explore his palace! He girded his sword about him; it was a scimitar of beautiful workmanship, and the scabbard was incrusted with precious stones.... From the court he passed into many wonderful rooms, one leading out of the other; there were rich carpets on the marble floors, and fountains played softly in the centre, the walls were inlaid with rare marbles; but he never saw a living soul.

In the last hour Amyntas had become fully alive to his great importance, and carried himself accordingly. He took long, dignified steps, and held one hand on the jewelled hilt of his sword, with his elbows stuck out at right angles to his body; his head was thrown back proudly and his nostrils dilated with appropriate scorn. At last he came to a door closed by a curtain; he raised it. But he started back and was so surprised that he found no words to express his emotions. Four maidens were sitting in the room, more beautiful than he had thought possible in his most extravagant dreams. The gods had evidently not intended Amyntas for single blessedness.... The young persons appeared not to have noticed him. Two of them were seated on rugs playing a languid game of chess, the others were lazily smoking cigarettes.

'Mate!' murmured one of the players.

'Oh!' sighed the other, yawning, 'another game finished! That makes five million and twenty-three games against your five million and seventy-nine.'

They all yawned.

But Amyntas felt he must give notice of his presence, and suddenly remembering an expression he had learnt on board ship, he put on a most ferocious look and cried out,

'Shiver my timbers!'

The maidens turned towards him with a little cry, but they quickly recovered themselves and one of them came towards him.

'You speak like a king's son, oh youth!' she said.

There was a moment's hesitation, and the lady, with a smile, added, 'Oh, ardently expected one, you are a compendium of the seven excellences!'

Then they all began to pay him compliments, each one capping the other's remark.

'You have a face like the full moon, oh youth; your eyes are the eyes of the gazelle; your walk is like the gait of the mountain partridge; your chin is as an apple; your cheeks are pomegranates.'

But Amyntas interrupted them.

'For God's sake, madam,' he said, 'let us have no palavering, and if you love me give me some victuals!...'

Immediately female slaves came in with salvers laden with choice food, and the four maidens plied Amyntas with delicacies. At the end of the repast they sprinkled him with rose-water, and the eldest of them put a crown of roses on his hair. Amyntas thought that after all life was not an empty dream.

XIII

'And now, may it please you, oh stranger, to hear our story.

'Know then that our father was a Moor, one of the wealthiest of his people, and he dwelt with his fellows in Spain, honoured and beloved. Now, when Allah, whose name be exalted! decreed that our nation should be driven from the country, he, unwilling to leave the land of his birth, built him, with the aid of magic arts, this palace. Here he brought us, his four daughters and all his riches; he peopled it with slaves and filled it with all necessary things, and here we lived in peace and prosperity for many years; but at last a great misfortune befell us, for our father, who was a very learned man and accustomed to busy himself with many abstruse matters, one day got lost in a metaphysical speculation and has never been found again.'

Here she stopped, and they all sighed deeply.

'We searched high and low, but in vain, and he has not been found to this day. So we took his will, and having broken the seal, read the following, "My daughters, I know by my wisdom that the time will come when I shall be lost to you; then you will live alone enjoying the riches and the pleasures which I have put at your disposal; but I foresee that at the end of many years a youth will find his way to this your palace. And though my magic arts have been able to build this paradise for your habitation, though they have endowed you with perpetual youth and loveliness, and, greatest deed of all, have banished hence the dark shadow of Death, yet have they not the power to make four maidens live in happiness and unity with but one man! Therefore, I have given unto each of you certain gifts, and of you four the youth shall choose one to be his love; and to him and her shall belong this palace, and all my riches, and all my power; while the remaining three shall leave everything here to these two, and depart hence forever."

'Now, gentle youth, it is with you to choose which of us four you will have remain.'

Amyntas looked at the four damsels standing before him, and his heart beat violently.

'I,' resumed the speaker, 'I am the eldest of the four, and it is my right to speak first.'

She stepped forward and stood alone in front of Amyntas; her aspect was most queenly, her features beautiful and clear, her eyes proud and fiery; and masses of raven hair contrasted with the red flaming of her garments. With an imperious gesture she flung back her hair, and spoke thus,

'Know, youth, that the gift which my father gave me was the gift of war, and I have the power to make a great warrior of him whose love I am. I will make you a king, youth; you shall command mighty armies, and you shall lead them to battle on a prancing horse; your enemies shall quail before your face, and at last you shall die no sluggard's death, but pierced by honourable wounds, and the field of battle shall be your deathbed; a nation shall mourn your loss, and your name shall go down famous to after ages.'

'You are very beautiful,' said Amyntas, 'but I am not so eager for warlike exploits as when I wandered through the green lanes of my native land. Let me hear the others.'

A second stepped forward. She was clad most gorgeously of all; a crown of diamonds was on her head, and her robes were of cloth of gold sewn with rubies and emeralds and sapphires.

'The gift I have to give is wealth, riches, riches innumerable, riches greater than man can dream of. Do you want to be a king, the riches I can give will make you one; do you want armies, riches can procure them; do you want victory, riches can buy it, all these that my sister offers you can I with my riches give you; and more than that, for everything in the world can be got with riches, and you shall be all-powerful. Take me to be your love and I will make you the Lord of Gold.'

Amyntas smiled.

'You forget, lady, that I am but twenty.'

The third stepped forward. She was beautiful and pale and thoughtful. Her hair was yellow, like corn when the sun is shining on it; and her dress was green, like the young grass of the spring. She spoke without the animation of the others, mournfully rather than proudly, and she looked at Amyntas with melancholy eyes.

'I am the Lady of Art; all that is beautiful and good and wise is in my province. Live with me; I will make you a poet, and you shall sing beautiful songs. You shall be wise; and in perfect wisdom, oh youth! is perfect happiness.'

'The poet has said that wisdom is weariness, oh lady!' said Amyntas. 'My father is a poet; he has written ten thousand Latin hexameters, and a large number of Greek iambics.' ...

Then came forward the last. As she stood before Amyntas a cry burst from him; he had never in his life seen anyone so ravishingly beautiful. She was looking down, and her long eyelashes prevented her eyes from being seen, but her lips were like a perfect rose, and her skin was like a peach; her hair fell to her waist in great masses of curls, and their sparkling auburn, many-hued and indescribable, changed in the sunbeams from richest brown to gold, tinged with deep red. She wore a simple tunic of thin silk, clasped at her waist with a jewelled belt of gold.

She stood before Amyntas, letting him gaze; then suddenly she lifted her eyes to his. Amyntas's heart gave a mighty beat against his chest. Her eyes, her eyes were the very lights of love, carrying passionate kisses on their beams. A sob of ecstasy choked the youth, and he felt that he could kneel down and worship before them.

Slowly her lips broke into a smile, and her voice was soft and low.

'I am the Lady of Love,' she said. 'Look!' She raised her arms, and the thin, loose sleeves falling back displayed their roundness and exquisite shape; she lifted her head, and Amyntas thrilled to cover her neck with kisses. At last she loosened her girdle, and when the silken tunic fell to her feet she stood before him in perfect loveliness.

'I cannot give you fame, or riches, or wisdom; I can only give you Love, Love, Love.... Oh, what an eternity of delight shall we enjoy in one another's arms! Come, my beloved, come!'

'Yes, I come, my darling!' Amyntas stepped forward with outstretched arms, and took her hands in his. 'I take you for my love; I want not wealth nor great renown, but only you. You will give me love-alluring kisses, and we will live in never-ending bliss.'

He drew her to him, and, with his arms around her, pressed back her head and covered her lips with kisses.

XIV

And while Amyntas lost his soul in the eyes of his beloved, the three sisters went sadly away. They ascended the stately barge which awaited them, and the water bore them down the long avenue of columns into the darkness. After a long time they reached the entrance of the cavern, and having placed a great stone against it, that none might enter more, they separated, wandering in different directions.

The Lady of War passed through Spain, finding none there worthy of her. She crossed the mountains, and presently she fell in love with a little artillery officer, and raised him to dignity and power; and together they ran through the lands, wasting and burning, making women widows and children orphans, ruthless, unsparing, caring for naught but the voluptuousness of blood. But she sickened of the man at last and left him; then the blood he had spilt rose up against him, and he was cast down and died an exile on a lonely isle. And now they say she dwells in the palaces of a youth with a withered hand; together they rule a mighty empire, and their people cry out at the oppression, but the ruler heeds nothing but the burning kisses of his love.

The Lady of Riches, too, passed out of Spain. But she was not content with one love, nor with a hundred. She gave her favours to the first comer, and everyone was welcome; she wandered carelessly through the world, but chiefly she loved an island in the north; and in its capital she has her palace, and the inhabitants of the isle have given themselves over, body and soul, to her domination; they pander and lie and cheat, and forswear themselves; to gain her smile they will shrink from no base deed, no meanness; and she, too, makes women widows and children orphans…. But her subjects care not; they are fat and well-content; the goddess smiles on them, and they are the richest in the world.

The Lady of Art has not found an emperor nor a mighty people to be her lovers. She wanders lonely through the world; now and then a youthful dreamer sees her in his sleep and devotes his life to her pursuit; but the way is hard, very hard; so he turns aside to worship at the throne of her sister of Riches, and she repays him for the neglect he has suffered; she showers gold upon him and makes him one of her knights. But sometimes the youth remains faithful, and goes through his life in the endless search; and at last, when his end has come, she comes down to the garret in which he lies cold and dead, and stooping down, kisses him gently, and lo! he is immortal.

But as for Amyntas, when the sisters had retired, he again took his bride in his arms, and covered her lips with kisses; and she, putting her arms round his neck, said with a smile,

'I have waited for you so long, my love, so long!'

And here it is fit that we should follow the example of the three sisters, and retire also.

The moral of this story is, that if your godfathers and godmothers at your baptism give you a pretty name, you will probably marry the most beautiful woman in the world and live happily ever afterwards…. And the platitudinous philosopher may marvel at the tremendous effects of the most insignificant causes, for if Amyntas had been called Peter or John, as his mother wished, William II. might be eating sauerkraut as peacefully as his ancestors, the Lord Mayor of London might not drive about in a gilded carriage, and possibly even Mr Alfred Austin might not be Poet Laureate….

DAISY

I

It was Sunday morning, a damp, warm November morning, with the sky overhead grey and low. Miss Reed stopped a little to take breath before climbing the hill, at the top of which, in the middle of the churchyard, was Blackstable Church. Miss Reed panted, and the sultriness made her loosen her jacket. She stood at the junction of the two roads which led to the church, one from the harbour end of the town and the other from the station. Behind her lay the houses of Blackstable, the wind-beaten houses with slate roofs of the old fishing village and the red brick villas of the seaside resort which Blackstable was fast becoming; in the harbour were the masts of the ships, colliers that brought coal from the north; and beyond, the grey sea, very motionless, mingling in the distance with the sky…. The peal of the church bells ceased, and was replaced by a single bell, ringing a little hurriedly, querulously, which denoted that there were only ten minutes before the beginning of the service. Miss Reed walked on; she looked curiously at the people who passed her, wondering….

'Good-morning, Mr Golding!' she said to a fisherman who pounded by her, ungainly in his Sunday clothes.

'Good-morning, Miss Reed!' he replied. 'Warm this morning.'

She wondered whether he knew anything of the subject which made her heart beat with excitement whenever she thought of it, and for thinking of it she hadn't slept a wink all night.

'Have you seen Mr Griffith this morning?' she asked, watching his face.

'No; I saw Mrs Griffith and George as I was walking up.'

'Oh! they are coming to church, then!' Miss Reed cried with the utmost surprise.

Mr Golding looked at her stupidly, not understanding her agitation. But they had reached the church. Miss Reed stopped in the porch to wipe her boots and pass an arranging hand over her hair. Then, gathering herself together, she walked down the aisle to her pew.

She arranged the hassock and knelt down, clasping her hands and closing her eyes; she said the Lord's Prayer; and being a religious woman, she did not immediately rise, but remained a certain time in the same position of worship to cultivate a proper frame of mind, her long, sallow face upraised, her mouth firmly closed, and her eyelids quivering a little from the devotional force with which she kept her eyes shut; her thin bust, very erect, was encased in a black jacket as in a coat of steel. But when Miss Reed considered that a due period had elapsed, she opened her eyes, and, as she rose from her knees, bent over to a lady sitting just in front of her.

'Have you heard about the Griffiths, Mrs Howlett?'

'No!... What is it?' answered Mrs Howlett, half turning round, intensely curious.

Miss Reed waited a moment to heighten the effect of her statement.

'Daisy Griffith has eloped, with an officer from the dépôt at Tercanbury.'

Mrs Howlett gave a little gasp.

'You don't say so!'

'It's all they could expect,' whispered Miss Reed. 'They ought to have known something was the matter when she went into Tercanbury three or four times a week.'

Blackstable is six miles from Tercanbury, which is a cathedral city and has a cavalry dépôt.

'I've seen her hanging about the barracks with my own eyes,' said Mrs Howlett, 'but I never suspected anything.'

'Shocking! isn't it?' said Miss Reed, with suppressed delight.

'But how did you find out?' asked Mrs Howlett.

'Ssh!' whispered Miss Reed, the widow, in her excitement, had raised her voice a little and Miss Reed could never suffer the least irreverence in church.... 'She never came back last night, and George Browning saw them get into the London train at Tercanbury.'

'Well, I never!' exclaimed Mrs Howlett.

'D'you think the Griffiths'll have the face to come to church?'

'I shouldn't if I was them,' said Miss Reed.

But at that moment the vestry door was opened and the organ began to play the hymn.

'I'll see you afterwards,' Miss Reed whispered hurriedly; and rising from their seats, both ladies began to sing,

O Jesu, thou art standing
Outside the fast closed door,
In lowly patience waiting
To pass the threshold o'er;
We bear the name of Christians....

Miss Reed held the book rather close to her face, being shortsighted; but, without even lifting her eyes, she had become aware of the entrance of Mrs Griffith and George. She glanced significantly at Mrs Howlett. Mr Griffith hadn't come, although he was churchwarden, and Mrs Howlett gave an answering look which meant that it was then evidently quite true. But they both gathered themselves together for the last verse, taking breath.

O Jesus, thou art pleading
In accents meek and low....

A-A-men! The congregation fell to its knees, and the curate, rolling his eyes to see who was in church, began gabbling the morning prayers, 'Dearly beloved brethren.' ...

II

At the Sunday dinner, the vacant place of Daisy Griffith stared at them. Her father sat at the head of the table, looking down at his plate, in silence; every now and then, without raising his head, he glanced up at the empty space, filled with a madness of grief.... He had gone into Tercanbury in the morning, inquiring at the houses of all Daisy's friends, imagining that she had spent the night with one of them. He could not believe that George Browning's story was true, he could so easily have been mistaken in the semi-darkness of the station. And even he had gone to the barracks, his cheeks still burned with the humiliation, asking if they knew a Daisy Griffith.

He pushed his plate away with a groan. He wished passionately that it were Monday, so that he could work. And the post would surely bring a letter, explaining.

'The vicar asked where you were,' said Mrs Griffith.

Robert, the father, looked at her with his pained eyes, but her eyes were hard and shining, her lips almost disappeared in the tight closing of the mouth. She was willing to believe the worst. He looked at his son; he was frowning; he looked as coldly angry as the mother. He, too, was willing to believe everything, and they neither seemed very sorry.... Perhaps they were even glad.

'I was the only one who loved her,' he muttered to himself, and pushing back his chair he got up and left the room. He almost tottered; he had aged twenty years in the night.

'Aren't you going to have any pudding?' asked his wife.

He made no answer.

He walked out into the courtyard quite aimlessly, but the force of habit took him to the workshop, where, every Sunday afternoon, he was used to going after dinner to see that everything was in order, and to-day also he opened the window, put away a tool which the men had left about, examined the Saturday's work....

Mrs Griffith and George, stiff and ill at ease in his clumsy Sunday clothes, went on with their dinner.

'D'you think the vicar knew?' he asked as soon as the father had closed the door.

'I don't think he'd have asked if he had. Mrs Gray might, but he's too simple, unless she put him up to it.'

'I thought I should never get round with the plate,' said George. Mr Griffith, being a carpenter, which is respectable and well-to-do, which is honourable, had been made churchwarden, and part of his duty was to take round the offertory plate. This duty George performed in his father's occasional absences, as when a coffin was very urgently required.

'I wasn't going to let them get anything out of me,' said Mrs Griffith, defiantly.

All through the service a number of eyes had been fixed on them, eager to catch some sign of emotion, full of horrible curiosity to know what the Griffiths felt and thought; but Mrs Griffith had been inscrutable.

III

Next day the Griffiths lay in wait for the postman; George sat by the parlour window, peeping through the muslin curtains.

'Fanning's just coming up the street,' he said at last. Until the post had come old Griffith could not work; in the courtyard at the back was heard the sound of hammering.

There was a rat-tat at the door, the sound of a letter falling on the mat, and Fanning the postman passed on. George leaned back quickly so that he might not see him. Mr Griffith fetched the letter, opened it with trembling hands.... He gave a little gasp of relief.

'She's got a situation in London.'

'Is that all she says?' asked Mrs Griffith. 'Give me the letter,' and she almost tore it from her husband's hand.

She read it through and uttered a little ejaculation of contempt, almost of triumph. 'You don't mean to say you believe that?' she cried.

'Let's look, mother,' said George. He read the letter and he too gave a snort of contempt.

'She says she's got a situation,' repeated Mrs Griffith, with a sneer at her husband, 'and we're not to be angry or anxious, and she's quite happy, and we can write to Charing Cross Post Office. I know what sort of a situation she's got.'

Mr Griffith looked from his wife to his son.

'Don't you think it's true?' he asked helplessly. At the first moment he had put the fullest faith in Daisy's letter, he had been so anxious to believe it; but the scorn of the others....

'There's Miss Reed coming down the street,' said George. 'She's looking this way, and she's crossing over. I believe she's coming in.'

'What does she want?' asked Mrs Griffith, angrily.

There was another knock at the door, and through the curtains they saw Miss Reed's eyes looking towards them, trying to pierce the muslin. Mrs Griffith motioned the two men out of the room, and hurriedly put antimacassars on the chairs. The knock was repeated, and Mrs Griffith, catching hold of a duster, went to the door.

'Oh, Miss Reed! Who'd have thought of seeing you?' she cried with surprise.

'I hope I'm not disturbing,' answered Miss Reed, with an acid smile.

'Oh, dear no!' said Mrs Griffith. 'I was just doing the dusting in the parlour. Come in, won't you? The place is all upside down, but you won't mind that, will you?'

Miss Reed sat on the edge of a chair.

'I thought I'd just pop in to ask about dear Daisy. I met Fanning as I was coming along and he told me you'd had a letter.'

'Oh! Daisy?' Mrs Griffith had understood at once why Miss Reed came, but she was rather at a loss for an answer.... 'Yes, we have had a letter from her. She's up in London.'

'Yes, I knew that,' said Miss Reed. 'George Browning saw them get into the London train, you know.'

Mrs Griffith saw it was no good fencing, but an idea occurred to her.

'Yes, of course her father and I are very distressed about, her eloping like that.'

'I can quite understand that,' said Miss Reed.

'But it was on account of his family. He didn't want anyone to know about it till he was married.'

'Oh!' said Miss Reed, raising her eyebrows very high.

'Yes,' said Mrs Griffith, 'that's what she said in her letter; they were married on Saturday at a registry office.'

'But, Mrs Griffith, I'm afraid she's been deceiving you. It's Captain Hogan.... and he's a married man.'

She could have laughed outright at the look of dismay on Mrs Griffith's face. The blow was sudden, and notwithstanding all her power of self-control, Mrs Griffith could not help herself. But at once she recovered, an angry flush appeared on her cheek bones.

'You don't mean it?' she cried.

'I'm afraid it's quite true,' said Miss Reed, humbly. 'In fact I know it is.'

'Then she's a lying, deceitful hussy, and she's made a fool of all of us. I give you my word of honour that she told us she was married; I'll fetch you the letter.' Mrs Griffith rose from her chair, but Miss Reed put out a hand to stop her.

'Oh, don't trouble, Mrs Griffith; of course I believe you,' she said, and Mrs Griffith immediately sat down again.

But she burst into a storm of abuse of Daisy, for her deceitfulness and wickedness. She vowed she should never forgive her. She assured Miss Reed again and again that she had known nothing about it. Finally she burst into a perfect torrent of tears. Miss Reed was mildly sympathetic; but now she was anxious to get away to impart her news to the rest of Blackstable. Mrs Griffith sobbed her visitor out of the front door, but, when she had closed it, dried her tears. She went into the parlour and flung open the door that led to the back room. Griffith was sitting with his face hidden in his hands, and every now and then a sob shook his great frame. George was very pale, biting his nails.

'You heard what she said,' cried Mrs Griffith. 'He's married!' ... She looked at her husband contemptuously. 'It's all very well for you to carry on like that now. It was you who did it; it was all your fault. If she'd been brought up as I wanted her to be, this wouldn't ever have happened.'

Again there was a knock, and George, going out, ushered in Mrs Gray, the vicar's wife. She rushed in when she heard the sound of voices.

'Oh, Mrs Griffith, it's dreadful! simply dreadful! Miss Reed has just told me all about it. What is to be done? And what'll the dissenters make of it? Oh, dear, it's simply dreadful!'

'You've just come in time, Mrs Gray,' said Mrs Griffith, angrily. 'It's not my fault, I can tell you that. It's her father who's brought it about. He would have her go into Tercanbury to be educated, and he would have her take singing lessons and dancing lessons. The Church school was good enough for George. It's been Daisy this and Daisy that all through. Me and George have been always put by for Daisy. I didn't want her brought up above her station, I can assure you. It's him who would have her brought up as a lady; and see what's come of it! And he let her spend any money she liked on her dress.... It wasn't me that let her go into Tercanbury every day in the week if she wanted to. I knew she was up to no good. There you see what you've brought her to; it's you who's disgraced us all!'

She hissed out the words with intense malignity, nearly screaming in the bitterness she felt towards the beautiful daughter of better education than herself, almost of different station. It was all but a triumph for her that this had happened. It brought her daughter down; she turned the tables, and now, from the superiority of her virtue, she looked down upon her with utter contempt.

IV

On the following Sunday the people of Blackstable enjoyed an emotion; as Miss Reed said,

'It was worth going to church this morning, even for a dissenter.'

The vicar was preaching, and the congregation paid a very languid attention, but suddenly a curious little sound went through the church, one of those scarcely perceptible noises which no comparison can explain; it was a quick attraction of all eyes, an arousing of somnolent intelligences, a slight, quick drawing-in of the breath. The listeners had heeded very indifferently Mr Gray's admonitions to brotherly love and charity as matters which did not concern them other than abstractedly; but quite suddenly they had realised that he was bringing his discourse round to the subject of Daisy Griffith, and they pricked up both ears. They saw it coming directly along the highways of Vanity and Luxuriousness; and everyone became intensely wide awake.

'And we have in all our minds,' he said at last, 'the terrible fall which has almost broken the hearts of sorrowing parents and brought bitter grief, bitter grief and shame to all of us.'...

He went on hinting at the scandal in the manner of the personal columns in newspapers, and drawing a number of obvious morals. The Griffith family were sitting in their pew well in view of the congregation; and losing even the shadow of decency, the people turned round and stared at them, ghoul-like.... Robert Griffith sat in the corner with his head bent down, huddled up, his rough face speaking in all its lines the terrible humiliation; his hair was all dishevelled. He was not more than fifty, and he looked an old man. But Mrs Griffith sat next him, very erect, not leaning against the back, with her head well up, her mouth firmly closed, and she looked straight in front of her, her little eyes sparkling, as if she had not an idea that a hundred people were staring at her. In the other corner was George, very white, looking up at the roof in simulation of indifference. Suddenly a sob came from the Griffiths' pew, and people saw that the father had broken down; he seemed to forget where he was, and he cried as if indeed his heart were broken. The great tears ran down his cheeks in the sight of all, the painful tears of men; he had not even the courage to hide his face in his hands. Still Mrs Griffith made no motion, she never gave a sign that she heard her husband's agony; but two little red spots appeared angrily on her cheek bones, and perhaps she compressed her lips a little more tightly....

V

Six months passed. One evening, when Mr Griffith was standing at the door after work, smoking his pipe, the postman handed him a letter. He changed colour and his hand shook when he recognised the handwriting. He turned quickly into the house.

'A letter from Daisy,' he said. They had not replied to her first letter, and since then had heard nothing.

'Give it me,' said his wife.

He drew it quickly towards him, with an instinctive gesture of retention.

'It's addressed to me.'

'Well, then, you'd better open it.'

He looked up at his wife; he wanted to take the letter away and read it alone, but her eyes were upon him, compelling him there and then to open it.

'She wants to come back,' he said in a broken voice.

Mrs Griffith snatched the letter from him.

'That means he's left her,' she said.

The letter was all incoherent, nearly incomprehensible, covered with blots, every other word scratched out. One could see that the girl was quite distraught, and Mrs Griffith's keen eyes saw the trace of tears on the paper.... It was a long, bitter cry of repentance. She begged them to take her back, repeating again and again the cry of penitence, piteously beseeching them to forgive her.

'I'll go and write to her,' said Mr Griffith.

'Write what?'

'Why, that it's all right and she isn't to worry; and we want her back, and that I'll go up and fetch her.'

Mrs Griffith placed herself between him and the door.

'What d'you mean?' she cried. 'She's not coming back into my house.'

Mr Griffith started back.

'You don't want to leave her where she is! She says she'll kill herself.'

'Yes, I believe that,' she replied scornfully; and then, gathering up her anger, 'D'you mean to say you expect me to have her in the house after what she's done? I tell you I won't. She's never coming in this house again as long as I live; I'm an honest woman and she isn't. She's a -' Mrs Griffith called her daughter the foulest name that can be applied to her sex.

Mr Griffith stood indecisively before his wife.

'But think what a state she's in, mother. She was crying when she wrote the letter.'

'Let her cry; she'll have to cry a lot more before she's done. And it serves her right; and it serves you right. She'll have to go through a good deal more than that before God forgives her, I can tell you.'

'Perhaps she's starving.'

'Let her starve, for all I care. She's dead to us; I've told everyone in Blackstable that I haven't got a daughter now, and if she came on her bended knees before me I'd spit on her.'

George had come in and listened to the conversation.

'Think what people would say, father,' he said now; 'as it is, it's jolly awkward, I can tell you. No one would speak to us if she was back again. It's not as if people didn't know; everyone in Blackstable knows what she's been up to.'

'And what about George?' put in Mrs Griffith. 'D'you think the Polletts would stand it?' George was engaged to Edith Pollett.

'She'd be quite capable of breaking it off if Daisy came back,' said George. 'She's said as much.'

'Quite right too!' cried his mother. 'And I'm not going to be like Mrs Jay with Lottie. Everyone knows about Lottie's goings-on, and you can see how people treat them, her and her mother. When Mrs Gray passes them in the street she always goes on the other side. No, I've always held my head high, and I'm always going to. I've never done anything to be ashamed of as far as I know, and I'm not going to begin now. Everyone knows it was no fault of mine what Daisy did, and all through I've behaved so that no one should think the worse of me.'

Mr Griffith sank helplessly into a chair, the old habit of submission asserted itself, and his weakness gave way as usual before his wife's strong will. He had not the courage to oppose her.

'What shall I answer, then?' he asked.

'Answer? Nothing.'

'I must write something. She'll be waiting for the letter, and waiting and waiting.'

'Let her wait.'

VI

A few days later another letter came from Daisy, asking pitifully why they didn't write, begging them again to forgive her and take her back. The letter was addressed to Mr Griffith; the girl knew that it was only from him she might expect mercy; but he was out when it arrived. Mrs Griffith opened it, and passed it on to her son. They looked at one another guiltily; the same thought had occurred to both, and each knew it was in the other's mind.

'I don't think we'd better let father see it,' Mrs Griffith said, a little uncertainly; 'it'll do no good and it'll only distress him.'

'And it's no good making a fuss, because we can't have her back.'

'She'll never enter this door as long as I'm in the world.... I think I'll lock it up.'

'I'd burn it, if I was you, mother. It's safer.'

Then every day Mrs Griffith made a point of going to the door herself for the letters. Two more came from Daisy.

'I know it's not you; it's mother and George. They've always hated me. Oh, don't be so cruel, father! You don't know what I've gone through. I've cried and cried till I thought I should die. For God's sake write to me! They might let you write just once. I'm alone all day, day after day, and I think I shall go mad. You might take me back; I'm sure I've suffered enough, and you wouldn't know me now, I'm so changed. Tell mother that if she'll only forgive me I'll be quite different. I'll do the housework and anything she tells me. I'll be a servant to you, and you can send the girl away. If you knew how I repent! Do forgive me and have me back. Oh, I know that no one would speak to me; but I don't care about that, if I can only be with you!'

'She doesn't think about us,' said George, 'what we should do if she was back. No one would speak to us either.'

But the next letter said that she couldn't bear the terrible silence; if her father didn't write she'd come down to Blackstable. Mrs Griffith was furious.

'I'd shut the door in her face; I wonder how she can dare to come.'

'It's jolly awkward,' said George. 'Supposing father found out we'd kept back the letters?'

'It was for his own good,' said Mrs Griffith, angrily. 'I'm not ashamed of what I've done, and I'll tell him so to his face if he says anything to me.'

'Well, it is awkward. You know what father is; if he saw her.'...

Mrs Griffith paused a moment.

'You must go up and see her, George!'

'Me!' he cried in astonishment, a little in terror.

'You must go as if you came from your father, to say we won't have anything more to do with her and she's not to write.'

VII

Next day George Griffith, on getting out of the station at Victoria, jumped on a Fulham 'bus, taking his seat with the self-assertiveness of the countryman who intends to show the Londoners that he's as good as they are. He was in some trepidation and his best clothes. He didn't know what to say to Daisy, and his hands sweated uncomfortably. When he knocked at the door he wished she might be out, but that would only be postponing the ordeal.

'Does Mrs Hogan live here?'

'Yes. Who shall I say?'

'Say a gentleman wants to see her.'

He followed quickly on the landlady's heels and passed through the door the woman opened while she was giving the message. Daisy sprang to her feet with a cry.

'George!'

She was very pale, her blue eyes dim and lifeless, with the lids heavy and red; she was in a dressing gown, her beautiful hair dishevelled, wound loosely into a knot at the back of her head. She had not half the beauty of her old self.... George, to affirm the superiority of virtue over vice, kept his hat on.

She looked at him with frightened eyes, then her lips quivered, and turning away her head she fell on a chair and burst into tears. George looked at her sternly. His indignation was greater than ever now that he saw her. His old jealousy made him exult at the change in her.

'She's got nothing much to boast about now,' he said to himself, noting how ill she looked.

'Oh, George!'... she began, sobbing; but he interrupted her.

'I've come from father,' he said, 'and we don't want to have anything more to do with you, and you're not to write.'

'Oh!' She looked at him now with her eyes suddenly quite dry. They seemed to burn her in their sockets. 'Did he send you here to tell me that?'

'Yes; and you're not to come down.'

She put her hand to her forehead, looking vacantly before her.

'But what am I to do? I haven't got any money; I've pawned everything.'

George looked at her silently; but he was horribly curious.

'Why did he leave you?' he said.

She made no answer; she looked before her as if she were going out of her mind.

'Has he left you any money?' asked George.

Then she started up, her cheeks flaming red.

'I wouldn't touch a halfpenny of his. I'd rather starve!' she screamed.

George shrugged his shoulders.

'Well, you understand?' he said.

'Oh, how can you! It's all you and mother. You've always hated me. But I'll pay you out, by God! I'll pay you out. I know what you are, all of you, you and mother, and all the Blackstable people. You're a set of damned hypocrites.'

'Look here, Daisy! I'm not going to stand here and hear you talk like that of me and mother,' he replied with dignity; 'and as for the Blackstable people, you're not fit to, to associate with them. And I can see where you learnt your language.'

Daisy burst into hysterical laughter. George became more angry, virtuously indignant.

'Oh, you can laugh as much as you like! I know your repentance is a lot of damned humbug. You've always been a conceited little beast. And you've been stuck up and cocky because you thought yourself nice-looking, and because you were educated in Tercanbury. And no one was good enough for you in Blackstable. And I'm jolly glad that all this has happened to you; it serves you jolly well right. And if you dare to show yourself at Blackstable, we'll send for the police.'

Daisy stepped up to him.

'I'm a damned bad lot,' she said, 'but I swear I'm not half as bad as you are.... You know what you're driving me to.'

'You don't think I care what you do,' he answered, as he flung himself out of the door. He slammed it behind him, and he also slammed the front door to show that he was a man of high principles. And even George Washington when he said, 'I cannot tell a lie; I did it with my little hatchet,' did not feel so righteous as George Griffith at that moment.

Daisy went to the window to see him go, and then, throwing up her arms, she fell on her knees, weeping, weeping, and she cried,

'My God, have pity on me!'

VIII

'I wouldn't go through it again for a hundred pounds,' said George, when he recounted his experience to his mother. 'And she wasn't a bit humble, as you'd expect.'

'Oh! that's Daisy all over. Whatever happens to her, she'll be as bold as brass.'

'And she didn't choose her language,' he said, with mingled grief and horror.

They heard nothing more of Daisy for over a year, when George went up to London for the choir treat. He did not come back till three o'clock in the morning, but he went at once to his mother's room.

He woke her very carefully, so as not to disturb his father. She started up, about to speak, but he prevented her with his hand.

'Come outside; I've got something to tell you.'

Mrs Griffith was about to tell him rather crossly to wait till the morrow, but he interrupted her,

'I've seen Daisy.'

She quickly got out of bed, and they went together into the parlour.

'I couldn't keep it till the morning,' he said.... 'What d'you think she's doing now? Well, after we came out of the Empire, I went down Piccadilly, and, well, I saw Daisy standing there.... It did give me a turn, I can tell you; I thought some of the chaps would see her. I simply went cold all over. But they were on ahead and hadn't noticed her.'

'Thank God for that!' said Mrs Griffith, piously.

'Well, what d'you think I did? I went straight up to her and looked her full in the face. But d'you think she moved a muscle? She simply looked at me as if she'd never set eyes on me before. Well, I was taken aback, I can tell you. I thought she'd faint. Not a bit of it.'

'No, I know Daisy,' said Mrs Griffith; 'you think she's this and that, because she looks at you with those blue eyes of hers, as if she couldn't say bo to a goose, but she's got the very devil inside her.... Well, I shall tell her father that, just so as to let him see what she has come to.'...

The existence of the Griffith household went on calmly. Husband and wife and son led their life in the dull little fishing town, the seasons passed insensibly into one another, one year slid gradually into the next; and the five years that went by seemed like one long, long day. Mrs Griffith did not alter an atom; she performed her housework, went to church regularly, and behaved like a Christian woman in that state of life in which a merciful Providence had been pleased to put her. George got married, and on Sunday afternoons could be seen wheeling an infant in a perambulator along the street. He was a good husband and an excellent father. He never drank too much, he worked well, he was careful of his earnings, and he also went to church regularly; his ambition was to become churchwarden after his father. And even in Mr Griffith there was not so very much change. He was more bowed, his hair and beard were greyer. His face was set in an expression of passive misery, and he was extremely silent. But as Mrs Griffith said,

'Of course, he's getting old. One can't expect to remain young for ever', she was a woman who frequently said profound things, 'and I've known all along he wasn't the sort of man to make old bones. He's never had the go in him that I have. Why, I'd make two of him.'

The Griffiths were not so well-to-do as before. As Blackstable became a more important health resort, a regular undertaker opened a shop there; and his window, with two little model coffins and an arrangement of black Prince of Wales's feathers surrounded by a white wreath, took the fancy of the natives, so that Mr Griffith almost completely lost the most remunerative part of his business. Other carpenters sprang into existence and took away much of the trade.

'I've no patience with him,' said Mrs Griffith, of her husband. 'He lets these newcomers come along and just take the bread out of his hands. Oh, if I was a man, I'd make things different, I can tell you! He doesn't seem to care.'...

At last, one day George came to his mother in a state of tremendous excitement.

'I say, mother, you know the pantomime they've got at Tercanbury this week?'

'Yes.'

'Well, the principal boy's Daisy.'

Mrs Griffith sank into a chair, gasping.

'Harry Ferne's been, and he recognised her at once. It's all over the town.'

Mrs Griffith, for the first time in her life, was completely at a loss for words.

'To-morrow's the last night,' added her son, after a little while, 'and all the Blackstable people are going.'

'To think that this should happen to me!' said Mrs Griffith, distractedly. 'What have I done to deserve it? Why couldn't it happen to Mrs Garman or Mrs Jay? If the Lord had seen fit to bring it upon them, well, I shouldn't have wondered.'

'Edith wants us to go,' said George, Edith was his wife.

'You don't mean to say you're going, with all the Blackstable people there?'

'Well, Edith says we ought to go, just to show them we don't care.'

'Well, I shall come too!' cried Mrs Griffith.

IX

Next evening half Blackstable took the special train to Tercanbury, which had been put on for the pantomime, and there was such a crowd at the doors that the impresario half thought of extending his stay. The Rev. Charles Gray and Mrs Gray were there, also James, their nephew. Mr Gray had some scruples about going to a theatre, but his wife said a pantomime was quite different; besides, curiosity may gently enter even a clerical bosom. Miss Reed was there in black satin, with her friend Mrs Howlett; Mrs Griffith sat in the middle of the stalls, flanked by her dutiful son and her daughter-in-law; and George searched for female beauty with his opera-glass, which is quite the proper thing to do on such occasions....

The curtain went up, and the villagers of Dick Whittington's native place sang a chorus.

'Now she's coming,' whispered George.

All those Blackstable hearts stood still. And Daisy, as Dick Whittington, bounded on the stage, in flesh-coloured tights, with particularly scanty trunks, and her bodice, rather low. The vicar's nephew sniggered, and Mrs Gray gave him a reproachful glance; all the other Blackstable people looked pained; Miss Reed blushed. But as Daisy waved her hand and gave a kick, the audience broke out into prolonged applause; Tercanbury people have no moral sense, although Tercanbury is a cathedral city.

Daisy began to sing,

I'm a jolly sort of boy, tol, lol,
And I don't care a damn who knows it.
I'm fond of every joy, tol, lol,
As you may very well suppose it.
Tol, lol, lol,
Tol, lol, lol.

Then the audience, the audience of a cathedral city, as Mr Gray said, took up the refrain,

Tol, lol, lol,
Tol, lol, lol.

However, the piece went on to the bitter end, and Dick Whittington appeared in many different costumes and sang many songs, and kicked many kicks, till he was finally made Lord Mayor in tights.

Ah, it was an evening of bitter humiliation for Blackstable people. Some of them, as Miss Reed said, behaved scandalously; they really appeared to enjoy it. And even George laughed at some of the jokes the cat made, though his wife and his mother sternly reproved him.

'I'm ashamed of you, George, laughing at such a time!' they said.

Afterwards the Grays and Miss Reed got into the same railway carriage with the Griffiths.

'Well, Mrs Griffith,' said the vicar's wife, 'what do you think of your daughter now?'

'Mrs Gray,' replied Mrs Griffith, solemnly, 'I haven't got a daughter.'

'That's a very proper spirit in which to look at it,' answered the lady.... 'She was simply covered with diamonds.'

'They must be worth a fortune,' said Miss Reed.

'Oh, I daresay they're not real,' said Mrs Gray; 'at that distance and with the lime-light, you know, it's very difficult to tell.'

'I'm sorry to say,' said Mrs Griffith, with some asperity, feeling the doubt almost an affront to her, 'I'm sorry to say that I know they're real.'

The ladies coughed discreetly, scenting a little scandalous mystery which they must get out of Mrs Griffith at another opportunity.

'My nephew James says she earns at least thirty or forty pounds a week.'

Miss Reed sighed at the thought of such depravity.

'It's very sad,' she remarked, 'to think of such things happening to a fellow-creature.'...

'But what I can't understand,' said Mrs Gray, next morning, at the breakfast-table, 'is how she got into such a position. We all know that at one time she was to be seen in, well, in a very questionable place, at an hour which left no doubt about her, her means of livelihood. I must say I thought she was quite lost.'...

'Oh, well, I can tell you that easily enough,' replied her nephew. 'She's being kept by Sir Somebody Something, and he's running the show for her.'

'James, I wish you would be more careful about your language. It's not necessary to call a spade a spade, and you can surely find a less objectionable expression to explain the relationship between the persons.... Don't you remember his name?'

'No; I heard it, but I've really forgotten.'

'I see in this week's Tercanbury Times that there's a Sir Herbert Ously-Farrowham staying at the "George" just now.'

'That's it. Sir Herbert Ously-Farrowham.'

'How sad! I'll look him out in Burke.'

She took down the reference book, which was kept beside the clergy list.

'Dear me, he's only twenty-nine.... And he's got a house in Cavendish Square and a house in the country. He must be very well-to-do; and he belongs to the Junior Carlton and two other clubs.... And he's got a sister who's married to Lord Edward Lake.' Mrs Gray closed the book and held it with a finger to mark the place, like a Bible. 'It's very sad to think of the dissipation of so many members of the aristocracy. It sets such a bad example to the lower classes.'

X   .

They showed old Griffith a portrait of Daisy in her theatrical costume.

'Has she come to that?' he said.

He looked at it a moment, then savagely tore it in pieces and flung it in the fire.

'Oh, my God!' he groaned; he could not get out of his head the picture, the shamelessness of the costume, the smile, the evident prosperity and content. He felt now that he had lost his daughter indeed. All these years he had kept his heart open to her, and his heart had bled when he thought of her starving, ragged, perhaps dead. He had thought of her begging her bread and working her beautiful hands to the bone in some factory. He had always hoped that some day she could return to him, purified by the fire of suffering.... But she was prosperous and happy and rich. She was applauded, worshipped; the papers were full of her praise. Old Griffith was filled with a feeling of horror, of immense repulsion. She was flourishing in her sin, and he loathed her. He had been so ready to forgive her when he thought her despairing and unhappy; but now he was implacable.

Three months later Mrs Griffith came to her husband, trembling with excitement, and handed him a cutting from a paper,

'We hear that Miss Daisy Griffith, who earned golden opinions in the provinces last winter with her Dick Whittington, is about to be married to Sir Herbert Ously-Farrowham. Her friends, and their name is legion, will join with us in the heartiest congratulations.'

He returned the paper without answering.

'Well?' asked his wife.

'It is nothing to me. I don't know either of the parties mentioned.'

At that moment there was a knock at the door, and Mrs Gray and Miss Reed entered, having met on the doorstep. Mrs Griffith at once regained her self-possession.

'Have you heard the news, Mrs Griffith?' said Miss Reed.

'D'you mean about the marriage of Sir Herbert Ously-Farrowham?' She mouthed the long name.

'Yes,' replied the two ladies together.

'It is nothing to me.... I have no daughter, Mrs Gray.'

'I'm sorry to hear you say that, Mrs Griffith,' said Mrs Gray very stiffly. 'I think you show a most unforgiving spirit.'

'Yes,' said Miss Reed; 'I can't help thinking that if you'd treated poor Daisy in a, well, in a more Christian way, you might have saved her from a great deal.'

'Yes,' added Mrs Gray. 'I must say that all through I don't think you've shown a nice spirit at all. I remember poor, dear Daisy quite well, and she had a very sweet character. And I'm sure that if she'd been treated a little more gently, nothing of all this would have happened.'

Mrs Gray and Miss Reed looked at Mrs Griffith sternly and reproachfully; they felt themselves like God Almighty judging a miserable sinner. Mrs Griffith was extremely angry; she felt that she was being blamed most unjustly, and, moreover, she was not used to being blamed.

'I'm sure you're very kind, Mrs Gray and Miss Reed, but I must take the liberty of saying that I know best what my daughter was.'

'Mrs Griffith, all I say is this, you are not a good mother.'

'Excuse me, madam.'... said Mrs Griffith, having grown red with anger; but Mrs Gray interrupted.

'I am truly sorry to have to say it to one of my parishioners, but you are not a good Christian. And we all know that your husband's business isn't going at all well, and I think it's a judgment of Providence.'

'Very well, ma'am,' said Mrs Griffith, getting up. 'You're at liberty to think what you please, but I shall not come to church again. Mr Friend, the Baptist minister, has asked me to go to his chapel, and I'm sure he won't treat me like that.'

'I'm sure we don't want you to come to church in that spirit, Mrs Griffith. That's not the spirit with which you can please God, Mrs Griffith. I can quite imagine now why dear Daisy ran away. You're no Christian.'

'I'm sure I don't care what you think, Mrs Gray, but I'm as good as you are.'

'Will you open the door for me, Mrs Griffith?' said Mrs Gray, with outraged dignity.

'Oh, you can open it yourself, Mrs Gray!' replied Mrs Griffith.

XI

Mrs Griffith went to see her daughter-in-law.

'I've never been spoken to in that way before,' she said. 'Fancy me not being a Christian! I'm a better Christian than Mrs Gray, any day. I like Mrs Gray, with the airs she gives herself, as if she'd got anything to boast about!... No, Edith, I've said it, and I'm not the woman to go back on what I've said, I'll not go to church again. From this day I go to chapel.'

But George came to see his mother a few days later.

'Look here, mother, Edith says you'd better forgive Daisy now.'

'George,' cried his mother, 'I've only done my duty all through, and if you think it's my duty to forgive my daughter now she's going to enter the bonds of holy matrimony, I will do so. No one can say that I'm not a Christian, and I haven't said the Lord's Prayer night and morning ever since I remember for nothing.'

Mrs Griffith sat down to write, looking up to her son for inspiration.

'Dearest Daisy!' he said.

'No, George,' she replied, 'I'm not going to cringe to my daughter, although she is going to be a lady; I shall simply say, "Daisy."'

The letter was very dignified, gently reproachful, for Daisy had undoubtedly committed certain peccadilloes, although she was going to be a baronet's wife; but still it was completely forgiving, and Mrs Griffith signed herself, 'Your loving and forgiving mother, whose heart you nearly broke.'

But the letter was not answered, and a couple of weeks later the same Sunday paper contained an announcement of the date of the marriage and the name of the church. Mrs Griffith wrote a second time.

'MY DARLING DAUGHTER, I am much surprised at receiving no answer to my long letter. All is forgiven. I should so much like to see you again before I die, and to have you married from your father's house. All is forgiven. Your loving mother,

'MARY ANN GRIFFITH.'

This time the letter was returned unopened.

'George,' cried Mrs Griffith, 'she's got her back up.'

'And the wedding's to-morrow,' he replied.

'It's most awkward, George. I've told all the Blackstable people that I've forgiven her and that Sir Herbert has written to say he wants to make my acquaintance. And I've got a new dress on purpose to go to the wedding. Oh! she's a cruel and exasperating thing, George; I never liked her. You were always my favourite.'

'Well, I do think she's not acting as she should,' replied George. 'And I'm sure I don't know what's to be done.'

But Mrs Griffith was a woman who made up her mind quickly.

'I shall go up to town and see her myself, George; and you must come too.'

'I'll come up with you, mother, but you'd better go to her alone, because I expect she's not forgotten the last time I saw her.'

They caught a train immediately, and having arrived at Daisy's house, Mrs Griffith went up the steps while George waited in a neighbouring public-house. The door was opened by a smart maid, much smarter than the Vicarage maid at Blackstable, as Mrs Griffith remarked with satisfaction. On finding that Daisy was at home, she sent up a message to ask if a lady could see her.

The maid returned.

'Would you give your name, madam? Miss Griffith cannot see you without.'

Mrs Griffith had foreseen the eventuality, and, unwilling to give her card, had written another little letter, using Edith as amanuensis, so that Daisy should at least open it. She sent it up. In a few minutes the maid came down again.

'There's no answer,' and she opened the door for Mrs Griffith to go out.

That lady turned very red. Her first impulse was to make a scene and call the housemaid to witness how Daisy treated her own mother; but immediately she thought how undignified she would appear in the maid's eyes. So she went out like a lamb....

She told George all about it as they sat in the private bar of the public-house, drinking a little Scotch whisky.

'All I can say,' she remarked, 'is that I hope she'll never live to repent it. Fancy treating her own mother like that!

'But I shall go to the wedding; I don't care. I will see my own daughter married.'

That had been her great ambition, and she would have crawled before Daisy to be asked to the ceremony.... But George dissuaded her from going uninvited. There were sure to be one or two Blackstable people present, and they would see that she was there as a stranger; the humiliation would be too great.

'I think she's an ungrateful girl,' said Mrs Griffith, as she gave way and allowed George to take her back to Blackstable.

XII

But the prestige of the Griffiths diminished. Everyone in Blackstable came to the conclusion that the new Lady Ously-Farrowham had been very badly treated by her relatives, and many young ladies said they would have done just the same in her place. Also Mrs Gray induced her husband to ask Griffith to resign his churchwardenship.

'You know, Mr Griffith,' said the vicar, deprecatingly, 'now that your wife goes to chapel I don't think we can have you as churchwarden any longer; and besides, I don't think you've behaved to your daughter in a Christian way.'

It was in the carpenter's shop; the business had dwindled till Griffith only kept one man and a boy; he put aside the saw he was using.

'What I've done to my daughter, I'm willing to take the responsibility for; I ask no one's advice and I want no one's opinion; and if you think I'm not fit to be churchwarden you can find someone else better.'

'Why don't you make it up with your daughter, Griffith?'

'Mind your own business!'

The carpenter had brooded and brooded over his sorrow till now his daughter's name roused him to fury. He had even asserted a little authority over his wife, and she dared not mention her daughter before him. Daisy's marriage had seemed like the consummation of her shame; it was vice riding triumphant in a golden chariot....

But the name of Lady Ously-Farrowham was hardly ever out of her mother's lips; and she spent a good deal more money in her dress to keep up her dignity.

'Why, that's another new dress you've got on!' said a neighbour.

'Yes,' said Mrs Griffith, complacently, 'you see we're in quite a different position now. I have to think of my daughter, Lady Ously-Farrowham. I don't want her to be ashamed of her mother. I had such a nice long letter from her the other day. She's so happy with Sir Herbert. And Sir Herbert's so good to her.' ...

'Oh, I didn't know you were.' ...

'Oh, yes! Of course she was a little, well, a little wild when she was a girl, but I've forgiven that. It's her father won't forgive her. He always was a hard man, and he never loved her as I did. She wants to come and stay with me, but he won't let her. Isn't it cruel of him? I should so like to have Lady Ously-Farrowham down here.' ...

XIII

But at last the crash came. To pay for the new things which Mrs Griffith felt needful to preserve her dignity, she had drawn on her husband's savings in the bank; and he had been drawing on them himself for the last four years without his wife's knowledge. For, as his business declined, he had been afraid to give her less money than usual, and every week had made up the sum by taking something out of the bank. George only earned a pound a week, he had been made clerk to a coal merchant by his mother, who thought that more genteel than carpentering, and after his marriage he had constantly borrowed from his parents. At last Mrs Griffith learnt to her dismay that their savings had come to an end completely. She had a talk with her husband, and found out that he was earning almost nothing. He talked of sending his only remaining workman away and moving into a smaller place. If he kept his one or two old customers, they might just manage to make both ends meet.

Mrs Griffith was burning with anger. She looked at her husband, sitting in front of her with his helpless look.

'You fool!' she said.

She thought of herself coming down in the world, living in a pokey little house away from the High Street, unable to buy new dresses, unnoticed by the chief people of Blackstable, she who had always held up her head with the best of them!

George and Edith came in, and she told them, hurling contemptuous sarcasms at her husband. He sat looking at them with his pained, unhappy eyes, while they stared back at him as if he were some despicable, noxious beast.

'But why didn't you say how things were going before, father?' George asked him.

He shrugged his shoulders.

'I didn't like to,' he said hoarsely; those cold, angry eyes crushed him; he felt the stupid, useless fool he saw they thought him.

'I don't know what's to be done,' said George.

His wife looked at old Griffith with her hard, grey eyes; the sharpness of her features, the firm, clear complexion, with all softness blown out of it by the east winds, expressed the coldest resolution.

'Father must get Daisy to help; she's got lots of money. She may do it for him.'

Old Griffith broke suddenly out of his apathy.

'I'd sooner go to the workhouse; I'll never touch a penny of hers!'

'Now then, father,' said Mrs Griffith, quickly understanding, 'you drop that, you'll have to.'

George at the same time got pen and paper and put them before the old man. They stood round him angrily. He stared at the paper; a look of horror came over his face.

'Go on! don't be a fool!' said his wife. She dipped the pen in the ink and handed it to him.

Edith's steel-grey eyes were fixed on him, coldly compelling.

'Dear Daisy,' she began.

'Father always used to call her Daisy darling,' said George; 'he'd better put that so as to bring back old times.'

They talked of him strangely, as if he were absent or had not ears to hear.

'Very well,' replied Edith, and she began again; the old man wrote bewilderedly, as if he were asleep. 'DAISY DARLING, ... Forgive me!... I have been hard and cruel towards you.... On my knees I beg your forgiveness.... The business has gone wrong ... and I am ruined.... If you don't help me ... we shall have the brokers in ... and have to go to the workhouse.... For God's sake ... have mercy on me! You can't let me starve.... I know I have sinned towards you. Your broken-hearted ... FATHER.'

She read through the letter. 'I think that'll do; now the envelope,' and she dictated the address.

When it was finished, Griffith looked at them with loathing, absolute loathing, but they paid no more attention to him. They arranged to send a telegram first, in case she should not open the letter,

'Letter coming; for God's sake open! In great distress. FATHER.'

George went out immediately to send the wire and post the letter.

XIV

The letter was sent on a Tuesday, and on Thursday morning a telegram came from Daisy to say she was coming down. Mrs Griffith was highly agitated.

'I'll go and put on my silk dress,' she said.

'No, mother, that is a silly thing; be as shabby as you can.'

'How'll father be?' asked George. 'You'd better speak to him, Edith.'

He was called, the stranger in his own house.

'Look here, father, Daisy's coming this morning. Now, you'll be civil, won't you?'

'I'm afraid he'll go and spoil everything,' said Mrs Griffith, anxiously.

At that moment there was a knock at the door. 'It's her!'

Griffith was pushed into the back room; Mrs Griffith hurriedly put on a ragged apron and went to the door.

'Daisy!' she cried, opening her arms. She embraced her daughter and pressed her to her voluminous bosom. 'Oh, Daisy!'

Daisy accepted passively the tokens of affection, with a little sad smile. She tried not to be unsympathetic. Mrs Griffith led her daughter into the sitting-room where George and Edith were sitting. George was very white.

'You don't mean to say you walked here!' said Mrs Griffith, as she shut the front door. 'Fancy that, when you could have all the carriages in Blackstable to drive you about!'

'Welcome to your home again,' said George, with somewhat the air of a dissenting minister.

'Oh, George!' she said, with the same sad, half-ironical smile, allowing herself to be kissed.

'Don't you remember me?' said Edith, coming forward. 'I'm George's wife; I used to be Edith Pollett.'

'Oh, yes!' Daisy put out her hand.

They all three looked at her, and the women noticed the elegance of her simple dress. She was no longer the merry girl they had known, but a tall, dignified woman, and her great blue eyes were very grave. They were rather afraid of her; but Mrs Griffith made an effort to be cordial and at the same time familiar.

'Fancy you being a real lady!' she said.

Daisy smiled again.

'Where's father?' she asked.

'In the next room.' They moved towards the door and entered. Old Griffith rose as he saw his daughter, but he did not come towards her. She looked at him a moment, then turned to the others.

'Please leave me alone with father for a few minutes.'

They did not want to, knowing that their presence would restrain him; but Daisy looked at them so firmly that they were obliged to obey. She closed the door behind them.

'Father!' she said, turning towards him.

'They made me write the letter,' he said hoarsely.

'I thought so,' she said. 'Won't you kiss me?'

He stepped back as if in replusion. She looked at him with her beautiful eyes full of tears.

'I'm so sorry I've made you unhappy. But I've been unhappy too, oh, you don't know what I've gone through!... Won't you forgive me?'

'I didn't write the letter,' he repeated hoarsely; 'they stood over me and made me.'

Her lips trembled, but with an effort she commanded herself. They looked at one another steadily, it seemed for a very long time; in his eyes was the look of a hunted beast.... At last she turned away without saying anything more, and left him.

In the next room the three were anxiously waiting. She contemplated them a moment, and then, sitting down, asked about the affairs. They explained how things were.

'I talked to my husband about it,' she said; 'he's proposed to make you an allowance so that you can retire from business.'

'Oh, that's Sir Herbert all over,' said Mrs Griffith, greasily, she knew nothing about him but his name!

'How much do you think you could live on?' asked Daisy.

Mrs Griffith looked at George and then at Edith. What should they ask? Edith and George exchanged a glance; they were in agonies lest Mrs Griffith should demand too little.

'Well,' said that lady, at last, with a little cough of uncertainty, 'in our best years we used to make four pounds a week out of the business, didn't we, George?'

'Quite that!' answered he and his wife, in a breath.

'Then, shall I tell my husband that if he allows you five pounds a week you will be able to live comfortably?'

'Oh, that's very handsome!' said Mrs Griffith.

'Very well,' said Daisy, getting up.

'You're not going?' cried her mother.

'Yes.'

'Well, that is hard. After not seeing you all these years. But you know best, of course!'

'There's no train up to London for two hours yet,' said George.

'No; I want to take a walk through Blackstable.'

'Oh, you'd better drive, in your position.'

'I prefer to walk.'

'Shall George come with you?'

'I prefer to walk alone.'

Then Mrs Griffith again enveloped her daughter in her arms, and told her she had always loved her and that she was her only daughter; after which, Daisy allowed herself to be embraced by her brother and his wife. Finally they shut the door on her and watched her from the window walk slowly down the High Street.

'If you'd asked it, I believe she'd have gone up to six quid a week,' said George.

XV

Daisy walked down the High Street slowly, looking at the houses she remembered, and her lips quivered a little; at every step smells blew across to her full of memories, the smell of a tannery, the blood smell of a butcher's shop, the sea-odour from a shop of fishermen's clothes.... At last she came on to the beach, and in the darkening November day she looked at the booths she knew so well, the boats drawn up for the winter, whose names she knew, whose owners she had known from her childhood; she noticed the new villas built in her absence. And she looked at the grey sea; a sob burst from her; but she was very strong, and at once she recovered herself. She turned back and slowly walked up the High Street again to the station. The lamps were lighted now, and the street looked as it had looked in her memory through the years; between the 'Green Dragon' and the 'Duke of Kent' were the same groups of men, farmers, townsfolk, fishermen, talking in the glare of the rival inns, and they stared at her curiously as she passed, a tall figure, closely veiled. She looked at the well-remembered shops, the stationery shop with its old-fashioned, fly-blown knick-knacks, the milliner's with cheap, gaudy hats, the little tailor's with his antiquated fashion plates. At last she came to the station, and sat in the waiting-room, her heart full of infinite sadness, the terrible sadness of the past....

And she could not shake it off in the train; she could only just keep back the tears.

At Victoria she took a cab and finally reached home. The servants said her husband was in his study.

'Hulloa!' he said. 'I didn't expect you to-night.'

'I couldn't stay; it was awful.' Then she went up to him and looked into his eyes. 'You do love me, Herbert, don't you?' she said, her voice suddenly breaking. 'I want your love so badly.'

'I love you with all my heart!' he said, putting his arms round her.

But she could restrain herself no longer; the strong arms seemed to take away the rest of her strength, and she burst into tears.

'I will try and be a good wife to you, Herbert,' she said, as he kissed them away.

W. Somerset Maugham - A Short Biography

William Somerset Maugham was born on 25th January 1874 to Robert Ormond Maugham and Edith Mary (née Snell). Robert was a lawyer dealing with the British Embassy's legal affairs in Paris, and he arranged for Maugham to be born at the Embassy on British soil to ensure his exemption from the law of conscription into the French army for all boys born on French soil. Given that both Maugham's father and grandfather were practitioners of law (Maugham's grandfather, also named Robert, co-founded the English Law Society) it was assumed that Maugham and his brothers would follow suit, and his brother's did; his eldest, Viscount Maugham, served as Lord Chancellor in 1938-39.

Maugham's deviation from the family career can perhaps be explained by his being raised effectively as an only child, for his three older brothers were already away at boarding school by his third birthday. Between the birth of the youngest of these three elder brothers and Maugham, Edith had contracted tuberculosis and the doctor had bizarrely prescribed childbirth as treatment, which led to Maugham's birth so long after that of his brothers. Of course, her pregnancy and Maugham's birth did little to alleviate her condition, so she had two more children after him, the last of whom was born on the 24th January 1882 and died the following day. Shortly thereafter on the 31st January Edith succumbed to her tuberculosis and died aged 41. Her early death had a profound effect on Maugham, and he kept her photograph at his bedside for the remainder of his life. This early childhood trauma was compounded by the death of his father from cancer two years later. Maugham was sent to Kent where his uncle, Henry MacDonald Maugham, was Vicar of Whitstable.

Maugham's time here was unhappy, for his home life with his uncle was emotionally damaging and Maugham had no better a time at The King's School, Canterbury, where he was teased for his poor English, French having been his first language as a child, and his diminutive stature. The combination of the loss of his parents, the cruelty he encountered from his uncle and the bullying at school manifested itself in a sporadic stammer, brought on by certain moods and circumstances, and which lasted his whole life. Despite this speech impediment, or perhaps in direct opposition to it, he developed a talent for pithy, cutting repartee and character assassination, usually directed at those who upset or displeased him. By the age of sixteen Maugham had had enough, and flatly refused to return to The King's School, and his uncle was happy for him to travel to Heidelberg University in Germany where he studied literature, philosophy and German. The year he spent there provided the opportunity for both literary and sexual awakenings. The literary came in the form of Maugham's first book, a biography of the Prussian-born Jewish composer Giacomo Meyerbeer, while the sexual came in the form of John Ellingham Brooks, an Englishman.

Maugham returned to England with increased confidence, and his uncle secured him a position in an accountant's office. This proved unsatisfactory, however, and so he gave it up after a month in favour of a return to Whitstable. It was now that he made the conscious decision to divert from the legal path laid before him by his grandfather, father and brothers, and so his uncle set to finding Maugham a new profession. The church was discarded owing to his stammer seeming ridiculous, and Henry Maugham's opinion that the recent law requiring civil service applicants pass an entrance exam before consideration meant it was no longer the career of gentlemen saw it rejected. At the suggestion of the local doctor, Henry Maugham resolved upon the medical profession. Though Maugham had developed such an interest in writing that anything but authorship was unsuitable, he was not yet of age and so elected to keep this from his uncle, which resulted in five years spent at St Thomas's Hospital in Lambeth, London, where he studied medicine.

Despite medicine being so far removed from Maugham's ideal career as an author, he understood its importance and did not consider his years of study a waste, or stifling to his creativity. On the contrary, in fact, he would later recall its value, writing "I saw how men died. I saw how they bore pain. I saw what hope looked like, fear and relief." Furthermore, living in London was exciting, for he met people of every class, many of whom he would have had little chance of encountering otherwise. During his studies, he kept notebooks of literary ideas and ensured he sustained his interest in writing alongside his degree. The usefulness of his time in London became apparent when it formed the inspiration for his second book and first novel, *Liza of Lambeth*, published in 1897. In it he explores the factory working conditions he witnessed in Lambeth, the relationships between the workers and themes of hope, despair and the importance of human life, all of which he was able to observe both during his studies and while living in Lambeth. The great success of *Liza of Lambeth*, whose first print run sold out in weeks, enabled him to drop practicing medicine (for he had now qualified) and begin his chosen career as an author, to which he took "as a duck takes to water".

For the next twelve years Maugham traveled in search of creative inspiration to places such as Capri and Spain. He produced ten works in this time, though none achieved the same success as *Liza*. *The Making of a Saint*, in 1898, and *The Hero*, in 1901, passed fairly under the radar, though *Mrs. Craddock* received moderate attention in 1902. Maugham had difficulty finding a publisher for it, since the subject of its protagonist, the titular Mrs. Craddock, and her decision to marry beneath her status was considered potentially offensive to the readership. Eventually Maugham agreed to terms laid down by the publishing house Heinemann, that he remove some of these offensive passages, and it was published. *The Merry-go-round* (1904) and *The Bishop's Apron* (1906) weren't discouraging, though they still failed to match *Liza* for critical and popular acclaim. Maugham's fortunes changed in 1907 with the production of his first play, *Lady Frederick*, which was met with a very positive response. It was so positive, in fact, that over the following three years Maugham had eight plays which he had written between 1903 and 1910 in the theatre. This popularity was carried over to the publication of *The Explorer* (1908) which marked his return to novelistic form. A clear indication of the extent of his popularity can be found in a popular *Punch* cartoon which depicted Shakespeare looking at the West End billboards and biting his nails in anxiety at the repetition of Maugham's name.

Drawing on the experience of meeting the infamous occultist Aleister Crowley in Paris for his next novel, *The Magician* (1908), Maugham discovered the true weight of his popularity, for Crowley's critique of the novel and its treatment of the protagonist Oliver Haddo, indisputably based on Crowley himself, which was published in *Vanity Fair* magazine and accused Maugham of plagiarism, was largely ignored and Maugham's reputation escaped unscathed, perhaps even bolstered for his audacious attack on the behaviour and belief of such a mysterious and influential man. With this, and his success as a playwright, Maugham's popularity evolved into thoroughbred fame. By 1914 he had published ten novels and ten plays, and being too old for military service at the outbreak of the First World War, he returned to France where he served with the British Red Cross's Literary Ambulance Drivers, a group of twenty-four well-known writers including John Dos Passos and E.E. Cummings. Also numbering among the group was Frederick Gerald Haxton, a young man from San Francisco, who became Maugham's secretary, companion and lover until his death in 1944. Both men had been affected by the trial and imprisonment of Oscar Wilde, and so they kept their relationship secret. Haxton, however, was found by military policemen in a Covent Garden hotel room in 1915 in a homosexual act that was not buggery with another man, John Lindsall, and they were tried on the 7th December at the Criminal Justice Court at the Old Bailey under the same law which saw Wilde convicted. Unlike Wilde, however, both men were acquitted and Haxton and Maugham were able to continue their relationship.

Despite Maugham's time being largely occupied by the Literary Ambulance Drivers, he again ensured he continued his writing, completing and proofreading *Of Human Bondage* while off-duty at Dunkirk. It was published in 1915 and initially met with harsh criticism by both English and American critics. However, thanks to the influence of American novelist and critic Theodore Dreiser, who considered the novel a work of art of Beethovenian genius, the novel was resuscitated and it has never since been out of print. The novel's title came from a passage in Spinoza's *Ethics*:

"The impotence of man to govern or restrain the emotions I call bondage, for a man who is under their control is not his own master… so that he is often forced to follow the worse, although he see the better before him."

Many of the aspects of *Of Human Bondage* are considered autobiographical, such as the protagonist Philip Carey's club foot (comparable to Maugham's stammer, made evident in the way Carey is treated for it), the vicar and town of Blackstable are reminiscent of Whitstable, and Carey himself is in the medical profession. Though Maugham denied this autobiographical nature, he later wrote that "fact and fiction are so intermingled in my work that now, looking back on it, I can hardly distinguish one from the other."

In 1915, Maugham began a relationship with Syrie Wellcome, who at the time was the wife of Henry Wellcome, the pharmaceutical magnate. Together Maugham and Syrie had a daughter, who they named Mary Elizabeth Maugham, who was born in 1915. Meanwhile, Henry Wellcome sued Syrie for divorce and Maugham was named as the co-respondent. Following the decree absolute which was passed in May 1917, Maugham and Syrie married, and Syrie took Maugham's name to become Syrie Maugham. They began to refer to their daughter Mary as Liza, after the protagonist from Maugham's first novel. They had an unhappy marriage, however, and Syrie found she could not live with Maugham's frequent travels and continuing relationship with Haxton, and so they divorced in 1929.

Electing to suspend his military duties in France, Maugham returned to England in order to promote *Of Human Bondage*, though he was eager to return to assistance with the war effort. Being unable to return to the ambulance unit, Syrie made arrangements for him to be introduced to a highly ranking officer in the intelligence officers, known as "R", and he was subsequently recruited by John Wallinger. In late September 1915 Maugham was sent to work in Switzerland in operation with a network of several other British agents against the Berlin Committee. He used his career as a writer as a cover for his residence in Switzerland, and did continue to write. In 1916 Maugham began research for his next novel, *The Moon and Sixpence*, which he researched in the Pacific with Haxton, who proved indispensable as an extrovert character who was able to interact with the people who Maugham wished to use as inspiration. His experience in the Pacific would encourage further writing about the area, and in his later works he would document more thoroughly the last days of British colonialism in India, and that of Southeast Asia, China and the Pacific. Haxton remained key to these journeys and books.

By June 1917, Maugham had been asked by Sir William Wiseman, another officer in the British Secret Intelligence Service, to take on a mission to keep the Provisional Government in Russia in power and thereby keep Russia in the war. The main task was to counter German propaganda which was threatening to bring down this government. The mission was a failure and the Bolsheviks took control only two months after Maugham's arrival in the country, though he later wrote that, had he been able to get there some six months earlier than he had, he thought he could have succeeded. His experience with the SIS led to a collection of short stories following a sophisticated, gentlemanly spy, named *Ashenden: Or the British Agent*. Several of its characters are based on those he met during his service with the SIS, and it is plausible that these stories formed the basis for Ian Fleming's famous character James Bond.

Maugham collected his experiences from traveling in China and Hong Kong in 1920 in *On A Chinese Screen*, which he dedicated to his wife Syrie and featured some fifty-eight very short sketches, designed to be broadened into short stories and novels but which never were. He wrote *The Painted Veil* in 1925, and then in 1926 bought Villa Mauresque, which had 9 acres of land on the French Riviera at Cap Ferrat. He made this his home for the majority of the rest of his life, and here he hosted a vibrant and highly-regarded literary salon during the 1920s and 30s, while keeping up his prolific literary output. One of the best-known works from this period is *An Appointment in Samarra* (1933), which is based on an ancient Babylonian myth and which John O'Hara credits as a key creative inspiration for his own *Appointment in Samarra*. By the 1940s, the collapse of France and its German occupation, Maugham found himself unable to remain at Villa Mauresque. He became a refugee, albeit one of the wealthiest and most famous of the many displaced English-speaking writers of the time.

By this time, Maugham was in his sixties, and he spent the majority of the Second World War, firstly in Hollywood where he wrote several successful scripts and made some of the first significant money from film adaptations, and then in the south of the United States. While here he made speeches to the United States encouraging their involvement in the war. Haxton died in 1944, and Maugham quickly returned to England. He met and began a relationship with Alan Searle, whom he had originally met in 1928. Searle was young, from the Bermondsey slums, and had prior experience of being kept by older men. His experience of this meant he was able to prove a devoted companion to Maugham, although Searle did not equal Haxton's liveliness or passion. One of Maugham's friends observed "Gerald was vintage, Alan was *vin ordinaie*". They returned to Maugham's villa in 1946. Maugham wrote about his troubled love life, confessing "I have most loved people who cared little or nothing for me and when people have loved me I have been embarrassed... In order not to hurt their feelings, I have often acted a passion I did not feel."

His family life took a further turn for the worse and to the notorious when, in 1962, Maugham sold a collection of paintings of which some he had already assigned to his daughter Liza by deed. She sued him successfully, winning a judgement of £230,000, and Maugham responded by publicly disowning her and claiming not to be her biological father, instead adopting Searle as his son and heir. Soon after he attacked Syrie in his memoirs, claiming that Liza had been born before their marriage and that her father remained unknown. His literary reputation was not enough to weather this public storm, though, and he lost several of his friends and endured masses of public ridicule over the memoir. His reputation in tatters, Maugham was death another blow when Liza and her husband, Lord Glendevon, had the change to his will overturned by the French courts. Searle instead inherited £50,000 and the contents of Villa Mauresque, Maugham's manuscripts and the future revenue generated by thirty years of copyrights. Following this these thirty years, the ownership of the copyrights were passed on to the Royal Literary Fund. Maugham died in Nice in 1961, and his ashes were scattered near the Maugham library at The King's School, Canterbury. He has no grave.

www.ingramcontent.com/pod-product-compliance
Lightning Source LLC
Chambersburg PA
CBHW071412170626
46811CB00003B/1365